MORE MYSTERIES FROM THE
BERKLEY PUBLISHING GROUP . . .

DOG LOVERS' MYSTERIES STARRING HOLLY WINTER: With her Alaskan malamute Rowdy, Holly dogs the trails of dangerous criminals. "A gifted and original writer."—Carolyn G. Hart

by Susan Conant

A NEW LEASH ON DEATH	A BITE OF DEATH
DEAD AND DOGGONE	PAWS BEFORE DYING

DOG LOVERS' MYSTERIES STARRING JACKIE WALSH: She's starting a new life with her son and an ex-police dog named Jake . . . teaching film classes and solving crimes!

by Melissa Cleary

A TAIL OF TWO MURDERS	FIRST PEDIGREE MURDER	THE MALTESE PUPPY
DOG COLLAR CRIME	SKULL AND DOG BONES	MURDER MOST BEASTLY
HOUNDED TO DEATH	DEAD AND BURIED	OLD DOGS
AND YOUR LITTLE DOG, TOO		

SAMANTHA HOLT MYSTERIES: Dogs, cats, and crooks are all part of a day's work for this veterinary technician . . . "Delightful!"—Melissa Cleary

by Karen Ann Wilson

EIGHT DOGS FLYING	COPY CAT CRIMES
BEWARE SLEEPING DOGS	CIRCLE OF WOLVES

CHARLOTTE GRAHAM MYSTERIES: She's an actress with a flair for dramatics—and an eye for detection. "You'll get hooked on Charlotte Graham!"—*Rave Reviews*

by Stefanie Matteson

MURDER AT THE SPA	MURDER ON THE SILK ROAD	MURDER AMONG THE ANGELS
MURDER AT TEATIME	MURDER AT THE FALLS	MURDER UNDER THE PALMS
MURDER ON THE CLIFF	MURDER ON HIGH	

PEACHES DANN MYSTERIES: Peaches has never had a very good memory. But she's learned to cope with it over the years . . . Fortunately, though, when it comes to murder, this absentminded amateur sleuth doesn't forgive and forget!

by Elizabeth Daniels Squire

WHO KILLED WHAT'S-HER-NAME?	REMEMBER THE ALIBI	IS THERE A DEAD MAN IN THE HOUSE?
MEMORY CAN BE MURDER	WHOSE DEATH IS IT ANYWAY?	

HEMLOCK FALLS MYSTERIES: The Quilliam sisters combine their culinary and business skills to run an inn in upstate New York. But when it comes to murder, their talent for detection takes over . . .

by Claudia Bishop

A TASTE FOR MURDER	A DASH OF DEATH	DEATH DINES OUT
A PINCH OF POISON	MURDER WELL-DONE	

AND YOUR LITTLE DOG, TOO

MELISSA CLEARY

BERKLEY PRIME CRIME, NEW YORK

AND YOUR LITTLE DOG, TOO

A Berkley Prime Crime Book / published by arrangement with
the author

PRINTING HISTORY
Berkley Prime Crime edition / March 1998

All rights reserved.
Copyright © 1998 by The Berkley Publishing Group.
This book may not be reproduced in whole or in part,
by mimeograph or any other means, without permission.
For information address: The Berkley Publishing Group,
a member of Penguin Putnam Inc.,
200 Madison Avenue, New York, NY 10016.

The Penguin Putnam Inc. World Wide Web site address is
http://www.Penguinputnam.com

ISBN: 0-425-16242-7

Berkley Prime Crime Books are published
by The Berkley Publishing Group,
a member of Penguin Putnam Inc.,
200 Madison Avenue, New York, NY 10016.
The name BERKLEY PRIME CRIME and the BERKLEY PRIME CRIME
design are trademarks belonging to Berkley Publishing Corporation.

PRINTED IN THE UNITED STATES OF AMERICA

10 9 8 7 6 5 4 3 2 1

CHAPTER 1

Palmer, Ohio, in the chilly aftermath of an unseasonable October snowstorm, wasn't anybody's idea of paradise, and the alley between Third and Fourth avenues just off South Illinois Street wasn't the most scenic location in the city in the best of weather. To Jackie Walsh, it was about as far from where she wanted to be as she could imagine.

Though she'd lived in the midwest most of her life, as far as Jackie was concerned snow was something to be viewed from the other side of a double-paned window while holding a steaming mug of hot chocolate. As she crept on her hands and knees toward the battered metal Dumpster situated against the brick rear wall of the All Saints Rescue Mission, she wished with all her heart that she could be seeing it that way now.

"Come on, little guy," she coaxed, as the shivering terrier who had taken refuge in the dark space underneath the trash container backed up even further into the shadows. "Come on out. Please. I'm trying to help you." The little dog lowered itself to its belly on the icy pavement and whimpered, no doubt as miserable as she was, Jackie thought, feeling the icy water of a puddle of melted, dirty snow soaking through her knit gloves and the knees of her jeans.

The snowstorm had come down out of Canada the night before, pushing a mass of freezing air ahead of it, dumping

1

three inches of snow on the city and outlying areas, then clearing off suddenly and allowing temperatures to plummet below freezing for most of the night.

By morning temperatures had risen and some of the snow had melted off, but here in the alleyway, plenty remained to hamper Jackie's efforts and lower her body temperature. She shivered and rubbed her hands together, but she couldn't really say it made her feel any warmer.

She could see the glint of the terrier's frightened eyes in the darkness underneath the Dumpster, the only spot in the alley that was remotely dry, but no matter how far she stretched out her arm, the dog remained just out of her reach. Sighing, Jackie lowered herself to her stomach in the slushy snow and reached out again, gasping with shock as the wet snow penetrated her sweater. This time her frozen fingers connected with the furry little body.

The dog yelped. Jackie braced herself for a bite on the hand as she pulled her arm back gently, the scruff of the terrier's neck firmly grasped in her fingers. The bite never came, but her unwilling captive dragged his feet every inch of the way into the watery sunlight of the alley, growling and whimpering by turns. Finally, he was out, and Jackie wrapped her arms around him as he shivered uncontrollably.

Jackie had first heard the dog's pitiful cries as she walked by the alley on her way between Third and Fourth, heading back to her car from the Farmers' and Growers' Market, a string bag of fresh fruits and vegetables hanging from each hand, and a colorful bouquet of carnations, asters, zinnias, and daisies tucked under one arm.

Curious, she had walked between the tall red and brown brick buildings that characterized this neighborhood of downtown Palmer, looking for the source of the sound. When she found it, and the shivering tan-and-white wire-haired mutt who was making it, she knew she wouldn't be able to walk away and let the poor pooch find its own way home.

She'd set down the bags and the flowers, and proceeded to coax the dog into the light. Now, having dragged the resisting creature out from under its temporary hiding place, she stood up, took off her jacket and wrapped him up in it.

"Come on, pal. Let's go someplace and keep warm." Jackie held onto the trembling dog with one arm and brushed the worst of the alley's dirty moisture from the front of her clothing as she straightened up. She held him against her body with one hand and picked up her bags with the other, managing to stuff the bouquet precariously into one of the bags and scoop up all the string handles in wet, icy fingers that burned with cold.

"Now we've got it," she told her new canine acquaintance. "If we can just keep from dropping it." She was just turning away for the relative warmth of her car a short walk away, when she noticed the hand sticking out from a heap of frozen trash protruding from under the Dumpster lid.

"Oh. My. God." Jackie backed away slowly, unable to take her eyes from the sight of the stiff, bluish-gray fingers that reached up like the hand of a drowning man, as though grasping for whatever might keep death away, if only for another moment.

In this person's case, Jackie knew, whatever that was had remained out of reach. The body that belonged to this hand was well and truly dead. It wasn't as though this was the first dead body she'd ever seen by a long shot, though she always harbored a hope that each one might be the last. She clutched the little dog to her midsection and turned away, looking around desperately for the nearest phone booth.

Jackie watched from a distance as the evidence technicians, having photographed the body from every conceivable angle, lifted it from the trash container onto an ambulance gurney for its ride to the morgue.

They worked quietly, with only an occasional muttered comment, their breaths frosty in the morning air. One tech fastened small paper bags over the stiff, blue hands and fastened them securely with tape while another removed items from the pockets of the clothing and dropped them into another bag. Jackie watched a pocket knife, a length of light chain, a folded, yellowed piece of newspaper, a few rumpled dollar bills, and some loose change go into the bag.

How sad to have your life come down to such a few pitiful things, she thought. A pocketful of junk, really. And how did someone end up like this, with nowhere to go on a freezing night? Were there people who were just doomed to die in a frozen alley somewhere, or could something like this happen to anyone?

CHAPTER 2

"I should have known," said a weary voice above and behind her. Jackie turned to see Detective Lieutenant Evan Stillman of the Palmer Police Department, towering head and shoulders above her, even with those broad shoulders stooped in resignation. "Don't tell me you're the one who called this one in," said Evan, shaking his head in a gesture Jackie was all too familiar with from their past interactions.

"Well, yes, sort of," Jackie protested. "But I was just passing by . . ."

Evan held up his hand to ward off Jackie's explanation, which was just as well, she was sure. She wasn't sure how she was going to explain to Evan why she just happened to be involved in what might prove to be yet another murder only a few months after the last time she'd become part of an accidental investigation. She wasn't sure she knew why herself.

"Of course you were," he sighed. "Just passing by." Jackie didn't sense any real antagonism coming from the tall, dark-haired detective, just a sort of resigned weariness which she'd grown used to. She and Evan went back a long way, back to when she had been seriously romantically involved with another Palmer, Ohio police detective, Michael McGowan. Well, those days were long over now, but her relationship with the Palmer Police Department seemed doomed to continue apace.

"It's not like I try to get in your way," she reassured him. Evan had never been particularly crazy about Jackie's level of involvement with police affairs, but he'd always been at least polite to her, and sometimes very nearly friendly.

"Oh, you're not in my way, Jackie," Evan said. "It's just that I'd hoped I could have a quiet, uneventful week to get my new partner accustomed to the routine, that's all."

"New partner, huh? Someone from the Palmer force?"

"Out-of-towner. Bernie Youngquist, formerly with the Evansville force."

"Is that Bernie?" Jackie asked, pointing to the middle-aged man in a brown overcoat, wire-rimmed spectacles, and latex gloves, talking to one of the evidence techs.

Evan laughed. "Nope. That's Karl Ludwig from the Medical Examiner's office. One of Cosmo's guys. *That's* Bernie."

Jackie followed Evan's pointing finger to a slender, petite woman in dark wool slacks and a tweed blazer. Her pale blonde hair was drawn back from a perfect heart-shaped face into a figure-eight knot at the nape of her neck. She leaned over the body, which had been removed from the trash container and was now lying on a Medical Examiner's stretcher, and she seemed to be having some sort of discussion with the evidence techs. "Hey, Bernie!" Evan shouted.

The woman looked up and saw Evan and Jackie standing there. Peeling off her latex gloves and tossing them into a paper sack, she took her leave of the evidence team, then straightened up and walked toward them.

"Jackie Walsh," said Evan when she had arrived to stand near them, "this is Bernadette Youngquist, your faithful Palmer P.D.'s newest Detective. Bernie, allow me to present Jackie Walsh, an old friend of my former partner, Mike McGowan. Jackie's a Communications instructor at Rodgers University."

"Communications?" Bernie asked, cocking her head slightly.

"Film," said Jackie, by way of explanation.

"Oh, I love movies!" Bernie exclaimed. Her face broke into a wide, natural smile. "We'll have to get together and talk sometime." She held out her hand and Jackie shook it.

"Absolutely. I'm always ready to talk movies." She could hear herself being inane, but there was something about Bernadette Youngquist's exquisite perfection that made her feel more than a bit inadequate, and she had to admit it rattled her.

"Yeah, you and Jackie ought to get on just fine. Jackie loves cops," Evan volunteered. "Even her dog used to be a cop."

Bernie looked at her curiously.

"That would be Jake, my German Shepherd," Jackie explained. "He was a Police Service Dog with the Palmer Police Department in a previous life."

"That's great," said Bernie. "He must be awfully smart."

"He is. And very good at what he does, even though he doesn't do it for a living anymore."

"Jackie discovered our John Doe over there," Evan told his partner.

"Jane," said Bernie.

"Huh?"

"It's Jane Doe. Our stiff is a woman. About fifty to fifty-five, I'd say. A few personal effects—very little cash, no I.D."

"Cause?"

"Ludwig thinks it looks like exposure—maybe helped along by alcohol. That seems the most likely thing to me, but we can't rule out homicide, unfortunately. Well, that's Cosmo's department—we'll let the autopsy decide." She turned to Jackie. "Did you notice anyone else around when you discovered the body?"

Jackie remembered the terrier, which had curled up and fallen asleep on her arm inside the jacket. She unbuttoned two buttons carefully and pointed inside to the dog, who poked his nose up into the light and opened his mouth wide in a yawn. "Just him."

"Oh, gosh, look at him!" Bernie exclaimed. "Isn't he adorable? What kind of dog is that? Do you know?" she asked Jackie.

"I'm no expert," Jackie said, looking down at the scruffy little bundle in her coat, "but I'd guess two or three kinds of terrier. Maybe some Dachshund in there somewhere, too. Who knows?"

"What are you going to do with him?" Bernie wanted to know.

"Gosh, I hadn't thought much about that," Jackie admitted. "I think he must have belonged to the woman who died."

"What makes you think that?" Evan asked. He took a closer look at the dog.

"Oh, just the way he was acting, I guess. He seemed really determined not to leave the Dumpster, for one thing. Like he thought he had a good reason for being there."

"Yeah, I guess he could belong to Jane Doe," said Bernie thoughtfully. "He doesn't have any tags, though." She fingered the worn leather collar around the terrier's neck.

"Do you suppose he's a material witness?" Jackie asked her.

"To what?" Evan asked. "Some drunk crawling into a Dumpster, passing out, and freezing to death?"

"We don't know for sure that's what happened, Evan," Bernie reminded him.

Jackie was secretly glad it hadn't fallen to her to keep Evan Stillman safe from unwarranted assumptions. It looked like this new detective might just be the one to keep him on his toes a bit. Good for her. Besides, there was something not quite right about the whole picture, though Jackie couldn't quite put her finger on what that might be.

"So what now, ladies? Are we supposed to take a statement from your friend there?" Evan waved a hand in the direction of the dog.

"Let's just make sure it—he?"

Jackie nodded.

"Let's just make sure we know where he is in case we need him. If it does turn out to be murder, he might be able to give some clue as to the perpetrator."

"You think we're going to run a lineup for a dog?" Evan asked.

"Something like that," Bernie replied. "People usually identify from visual evidence, but a dog might be able to identify someone from their scent." She looked to Jackie for confirmation.

"I have it on expert authority that even an untrained dog has a nose about a million times more sensitive than a human's," she told Evan.

"So maybe he could be of help," said Bernie.

"It'd never stand up in court," Evan assured her, but Bernie wasn't paying any attention to him. She was scratching the terrier behind one ear while he uttered a high-pitched groan of pleasure.

"I suppose we could get him lodging at the city dog pound," she said reluctantly. "It's not the greatest place in the world, but it's better than the streets, I suppose."

"Well, you take care of it," said Evan. "I don't want anything to do with the whole hare-brained idea. This witness is all yours, Detective Youngquist."

"I really hate to think of him going to the pound," said Jackie.

"Well, he wouldn't have the same status as a stray," Bernie said. "He'd be a guest of the City of Palmer until it's decided whether or not the woman's death was attributable to foul play."

"And after that?"

"I'm not sure. I guess if her death was accidental, he'd be put up for adoption."

Jackie remembered a long-ago visit to the city dog pound—the noise and the gloomy lighting, and the air of hopelessness that seemed to pervade everything there. Maybe it was just her. Maybe the animals couldn't care less where they were as long as they got food and water and stayed warm, but it just didn't seem right somehow.

Jackie's own dog, a large black-and-tan German Shep-

herd her son had named Jake, had been a stray when he
came to Jackie and Peter, three years ago. His previous
owner had also died, shot to death in an alley much like
this one in spite of Jake's heroic efforts to save him. The
big Shepherd had turned up on Jackie and Peter's doorstep,
wounded, and they had taken him in. Later they had learned
of his career as a Police Service Dog, retired with honors
from the Palmer force.

What if circumstances had been different, Jackie wondered. Suppose instead of finding a good home with two
people who had learned to love him, Jake had ended up in
one of those dingy concrete-and-steel cages at the Palmer
City Pound?

Bernie Youngquist watched Jackie's face, seeming to
guess the emotions there. "Of course you could take him
home with you. I think we could make a special allowance
for that, seeing as how you're the one who found him. What
do you think, Evan?"

Evan shook his head. "Yeah, whatever."

"I don't think I should," said Jackie, with real regret.
"I've got a dog and a cat at my place now, and Jake's
about seventy times his size, and I'm not sure how they'd
take to one another. This little guy has been through so
much already. I'm just afraid it might be too much of an
adjustment for him."

"I'd take him myself," Bernie offered, "but I live in a
fifth-floor apartment. No pets allowed. Maybe the pound's
the best idea all around," she allowed, reluctantly.

"No, wait," said Jackie. "My . . . friend . . . owns a kennel. He'll board him."

"Are you sure?"

"Positive. He won't be able to resist him."

"I don't know if the city will pay for putting him in a
kennel," said Bernie, looking to Evan as if for confirmation.

"No," said Evan, holding up a hand as if to ward off
any more bright ideas, "and he's not getting his own hotel

room, either, unless you want to enroll him in the Witness Protection Program, Youngquist."

"Let me worry about it," said Jackie. "I think I can talk my friend into doing it as a public service."

CHAPTER 3

Jackie pulled her Blazer up in front of Cusack Kennels and turned off the engine. From somewhere not too far away, dogs barked. The terrier was curled up on her jacket on the passenger seat, happy as Larry, as her Grandfather Cooley used to say.

She hoped she was doing the right thing bringing him here. Tom Cusack, the owner of the former Mel Sweeten Kennels since the previous spring, was the current romantic interest in Jackie's life, and she knew he'd take the little fellow in if she asked him, but was it fair to ask? He had a business to run in the first place, and involving him in a possible murder case might not be the best thing for the future of their relationship in the second place.

Jackie was pretty crazy about Tom, though she went out of her way to avoid using the word ''love'' to describe her feelings. It was clear he felt the same, though he was less shy about coming right out and saying it. In fact, he'd been saying it a lot lately, and had even taken to suggesting they ought to move in together. Occasionally, he hinted at even scarier things, like marriage.

The thought tempted her greatly, and at the same time scared her half to death. She had only in the last six months ended one relationship, with an actor named Ronald Dunn, when he had flown off to a location shoot in eastern Europe.

Once she was out of the situation with Ronald it was easy to see that it had been largely pointless—the kind of thing people get into because they've got absolutely nothing better to do. She and Ronald had very little in common, and he was indifferent to Peter, who needed a more active father figure in his life. Jackie didn't think she'd ever make that particular mistake again, but then Tom was nothing like Ronald, thank God.

And he was nothing much like Michael McGowan, either, she thought, but the kinds of feelings Michael had brought out in her were the same kinds of feelings—the same deep and troubling emotions—that Tom Cusack stirred up. She might not want to use the word, but Jackie was sure about how she felt about Tom and how much he meant to her, and she knew how afraid she was that something would go terribly wrong with their relationship, the way it had with her and Michael.

And now she was here to ask him a favor, and to get him involved in her latest round of weirdness. Come to think of it, this probably wasn't the best idea she'd had this week. Maybe she should just go.

Before she could decide whether she ought to start up the car again and leave, she caught sight of Tom coming out of one of the kennel buildings and walking toward the car. He wasn't much taller than her, with dark hair and smoky blue eyes, and a smile that could stop traffic. That smile did things to her, and he was wearing it now as he approached the Blazer.

Jackie wrapped the terrier up in her jacket again, and stepped out of the car, returning his smile, but nervously. "I brought you a little something," she said as Tom kissed her cheek.

Tom stepped back and regarded the bundle in Jackie's arms. "I can tell it's not cookies, because it's wiggling," he said.

"You've obviously never eaten my cookies," Jackie quipped. "But you're right this time." She opened her jacket and brought out the squirming terrier. "He needs a place to stay."

Tom took the little dog from her, jacket and all, and lifted up its face. "For how long?"

Jackie hadn't actually thought about that part. "I'm not sure. I think his owner is dead."

"You're not sure if he's dead?"

"She. And I'm sure about the dead part, but not about the owner part."

"Maybe you'd like to start from the beginning," Tom suggested, "while we find an empty guest room for your friend here." He scooped up the terrier, scratching him behind his ears and making comforting sounds, and carried him to the boarding kennels a few yards away along a winding, tree-shaded path.

Jackie followed, wishing she had her jacket back as a cool breeze worked its way through her damp sweater, but the jacket was still wrapped around the foundling in Tom's arms, and probably covered in dog hair besides.

"Well, I was just coming back from Farmers' and Growers' with some fresh fruits and vegetables," Jackie began, "and I was walking toward my car on Illinois Street."

"Just minding your own business," said Tom with a half-smile, opening the door to the kennel compound. The sound of barking dogs grew louder in volume, a chorus of high yips, deep, booming barks, and everything in between.

"As a matter of fact, I was," said Jackie, following him inside. She tried not to sound defensive when she said it, but between Evan and Tom, it was getting to be a habit today. "And I was passing by an alley and I heard this dog. He was hiding under a trash dumpster, nearly frozen."

"And the dead owner?"

"Inside the dumpster. Only I didn't know that until I'd dragged this little guy out from under it."

"You discovered the body?" Tom turned to look at her in surprise.

"Yes," said Jackie hesitantly. Tom had only known Jackie for five months, and with one major exception was still mercifully unused to her propensity for finding herself in the middle of criminal investigations. Jackie had hoped he might remain unused to it. "But it might not be murder."

"Did I say anything about murder?"

"No, but admit it—that's what you were thinking, wasn't it?"

"Well, it crossed my mind. After what we went through last spring . . ."

Five months ago, just as Jackie and Tom were beginning to get acquainted, the two of them—and their teenage children—had become dangerously involved in one of Jackie's unofficial investigations. Tom hadn't been at all accustomed to that sort of thing, and although he'd been a terrific sport about it, he had made it perfectly clear he wasn't interested in playing detective again anytime soon. Jackie could certainly sympathize with that.

"Yeah, I know," she replied wearily. "But it's nothing like that, honest it isn't. We aren't going to have another night like that one."

"Yeah, that'd be a tough act to follow, all right," Tom agreed. "Let's not try."

Jackie and Tom walked down the wide aisles between the kennels, as dogs of all shapes, sizes, and colors greeted them with wagging tails and an occasional bark or whine.

Joseph, Tom's assistant, gave Jackie a wave as she passed by the bin where he was scooping kibble into hard plastic dog dishes. "Hi, Jackie," he called. "How's our boys?"

"They're fine," Jackie answered him. "Charlie's the new Emperor of Isabella Lane, but he still takes time out to make sure Jake keeps his ears clean."

"You tell 'em hi for me," said Joseph.

"I will."

Jackie liked Joseph—a sweet-faced young man with long, curly red hair. He was a great guy and wonderful with dogs and cats. He did a lot of the grooming and some of the training, in addition to feeding the animals and being an all-around assistant to Tom. He even lived here at the kennels, renting an apartment on the top floor of the house Tom shared with his daughter, Grania, in the 1920s farmhouse conveniently located yards from the kennels and office.

"They think the woman died of exposure," she explained when they had walked out of Joseph's hearing range. "She was homeless, and she may have crawled into a dumpster to go to sleep."

"Without her dog?"

"That's it!" Jackie exclaimed. "Of course!" The feeling of something not quite right she had experienced back in the alley with Evan Stillman and Bernie Youngquist suddenly made sense. "I knew there was something fishy about it. No one would take shelter from the cold and leave their dog outside to freeze!"

"Of course it might not have been her dog," Tom observed.

"I suppose that's true," said Jackie thoughtfully. "But I can't get over the feeling that he was. He was just so determined to stay under that trash container, almost as though he were guarding something. Or someone. Anyhow, Bernie thinks it might be best to keep the dog under wraps until they know whether there was any foul play involved."

"Who's he?" Tom asked

"Who's who?"

"Bernie."

"She. Bernadette Youngquist. A detective with the Palmer police force. You'll probably get to meet her before this is over. Anyhow I sort of volunteered you to look out for the dog. I know I probably shouldn't have, but it was that or the City Pound."

"I wouldn't wish that on a dog," said Tom.

"Exactly. Then you don't mind that I offered without consulting you?"

"Is that what's worrying you? No, I don't mind. I've got a few empty kennels. I'm not going to have to put someone's poodle out on the street to make room for him."

He paused near a pensive-looking basset hound and an energetic beagle, and opened the door to an empty kennel between them. Then he removed the jacket and set the dog down gently on the floor. "I'll just leave you here to get acquainted with the neighbors," he said. "Joseph will be in to check on you in a bit. Let's hope the poor woman died accidentally, and that all this'll be over soon," he told Jackie.

"Yeah. Let's hope."

They left the kennel building and walked back toward the office. Tom shook out the worst of the dog hair and held out the jacket. Jackie slipped her arms inside, and Tom settled it around her shoulders, giving her a warm hug in the process.

Jackie accepted the hug gratefully, settling back against Tom's chest with a sigh. "We can always hope."

CHAPTER 4

"Look at this, Mom." Jackie's red-haired thirteen-year-old son Peter laid a folder of papers out on the dining room table in front of her. "It's a Family History project I have to do this week for Social Studies. It's really kind of neat. Check it out."

Jackie and Peter's German Shepherd, Jake, perked up his ears at the sound of a familiar phrase. He got up from the living room floor where Charlie, the ginger kitten who had been a gift from Tom, had been chewing on one of his huge black ears. He walked over to the table to have a look at what was being "checked out." Charlie meowed once in halfhearted protest, then turned his attentions to his own grooming.

"You can check it out too, Jake," said Peter. "This is called a family tree. But don't let the word 'tree' give you any ideas, okay?"

He picked out one folded sheet of paper from the pile and proceeded to unfold it and show it to Jackie. "See, my name goes here in the middle, and yours and Dad's go here on either side of it. Then we have to fill it in as far back as we can on both sides." His finger traced over lots of little blank boxes linked to other boxes, branching out farther and farther from the center of a print of a spreading oak tree.

"I have to get all the names, and dates and places of

birth, and some other stuff,'' said Peter. ''I'll call Dad this weekend and find out what he knows about his side of the family.''

''Good luck finding him at home,'' said Jackie, and instantly regretted it. ''I'm sorry, Peter. I guess I'm still just a little angry at your father, even after nearly four years.''

''That's okay, Mom,'' said Peter, giving her a smile. ''I understand. Dad can be a real jerk sometimes. Most of the time,'' he amended with a wry grin. ''Sometimes I'm pretty ticked off at him, too.''

''Thanks, Sonny Boy. So what else do you need for this project?''

''That's the fun part,'' he said. ''I have to collect anecdotes.'' He pulled out some other forms. Jake, having decided that the discussion had nothing to do with food, a walk, or playing, went back over to the rug in the middle of the living room floor and abandoned himself to the tender mercies of Charlie.

''What kind of anecdotes?'' Jackie asked.

''Oh, you know—family stuff. Stories about people and interesting things they did. That kind of stuff—you know.''

''Sounds like a job for your grandmother,'' said Jackie. ''Why don't you give her a call and see if she wants to come over for dinner? Then we'll spread all this stuff out on the table after we've eaten, and see how far we can get with it.''

''That's a great idea. I'll go call.'' Peter headed for the stairs, his room, and his telephone, leaving the folder and papers scattered on the table.

''Ahem!'' Jackie intoned loudly enough to carry halfway up the iron staircase, where Peter stopped and looked back at her.

''Was that a Peter 'ahem'?'' he inquired, straight-faced.

''Good to know it's only taken you thirteen years to learn to recognize one,'' she told him. ''How about putting these papers somewhere out of the way until we need them, okay?''

''Oh, okay.'' Peter trudged back down the staircase and gathered up the papers, stuffing them into the folder with considerably less neatness than they had been put in the first time.

"This is such a great project," he said with real enthusiasm. "I can't wait to find out what kind of cool stuff my family did."

"When your great-great grandfather Costello came to this country from Ireland in 1867," said Frances, "he was on the run from the law."

"What?" exclaimed Peter.

"What?" Jackie echoed. She looked at her mother to make sure she hadn't been joking, but Frances Costello's face was perfectly straight. Her hazel eyes stared coolly into Jackie's.

"I said that your father's grandfather was a wanted man."

"That is so utterly cool!" Peter breathed.

"Peter!"

"What?!"

"You find out one of our ancestors was a criminal and you think that's cool?"

"Well, it's sure a lot more interesting than anything Isaac is likely to find out about his family," Peter insisted. Peter's relationship with his best friend, Isaac Cook, had a touch of caveman competitiveness to it, but Jackie figured it was probably just a normal part of their development. Guy stuff.

"And he wasn't a criminal," said Frances, "at least not the way you're thinking, Jacqueline."

"Well, precisely how was he a criminal, then?" Jackie wanted to know.

"Well, there was an uprising against the English in that year," said Frances. "The Irish had been rising up once every generation for nearly seven centuries at that point, but this one was one of the least successful of them all, and over almost before it started, because the English had inside information.

"When the shooting—what little there was of it—died down, Michael Costello's parents borrowed from their relatives and sent their young revolutionary across the ocean to America one step ahead of an order for his arrest by the English, and that was that. He went to live in the home of his cousin in New York, got a job with the railroad, married a girl from Kilmurry, County Clare, named Nuala Meaney, and raised nine children. He lived to be ninety-three.''

Peter picked up the tape player and checked carefully to be sure it was still recording. "That's terrific, Grandma,'' he exclaimed. "Why didn't you ever tell me any of that before?''

"Because this is the first time you've shown any interest in the subject,'' his grandmother told him. "I've got dozens of stories nearly as good as that one whenever you want to hear them.''

"If I know Peter, he's going to want to hear them all,'' Jackie commented.

"Of course I do,'' said Peter. "Especially if they're as interesting as that one.''

"Family stories usually get more interesting as the years go by,'' Frances commented. "Someday you'll be telling your grandchildren about the day your mother discovered a dead body while doing her vegetable shopping.''

"Yeah, I probably will, huh? Are you going to be in the papers and everything 'cause you found that dead woman?'' Peter asked his mother.

"I don't think so,'' she told him. "Try not to be too disappointed.''

"Oh, that's okay, Mom. I know it happened, and knowing you, none of my friends will have any problem believing it's true.'' He smiled happily. "This family stuff is really great, isn't it?''

"Well, I always thought so,'' Jackie told him, "but I'll confess that until tonight I hadn't heard the one about my great-grandfather the fugitive.''

"Political dissident, Jacqueline,'' Frances corrected. "Your father never seemed to want to discuss it with you, but I don't see the harm. Now what else do you need for this report of yours, Grandson dear?''

"There's some points I have to cover besides the names and dates and stuff like that,'' he said, leafing through the pile of papers that had spilled out of his file folder and now littered the dining table amidst the dessert dishes and coffee cups Jackie hadn't bothered to remove yet. He pulled out a list and referred to it. "For instance, what language did my ancestors speak before they came to America?"

"Well, when the Shannons and the Cooleys—my parents' parents—left Ireland, nearly everyone spoke Irish. The English were already trying to put an end to that, but they hadn't had a lot of success yet."

"I don't get it," Peter told his grandmother. "Why didn't they want people to speak their own language?"

"It's all about colonialism," Frances said, "something the English did remarkably well. And if you've got several hours to kill some day I'll explain how they did it to the Irish. It's not at all a happy story, I'm afraid."

"You're going to make a rebel out of my thirteen-year-old son," Jackie warned halfheartedly.

"Nonsense, Jacqueline," her mother protested, "all thirteen-year-olds are rebels at heart. I'm just giving him some education about his heritage, that's all."

"I do want to hear it all sometime," Peter told his grandmother, "but for now just tell me about the language part."

"Well, in the early part of the last century the English government established state schools in Ireland to teach the children to speak English, and punished them if they spoke Irish."

"You mean, like standing in the corner kind of punished?"

"I mean like getting beaten kind of punished," Frances assured him. "The children wore sticks hung on a string around their necks, and the teacher would put a notch in the string every time the child said anything in Irish. When there were a certain number of marks on the stick, the child got a beating."

"Seems like a pretty extreme way to teach a foreign language," Peter observed. "Don't mention it to my French teacher. Did all the kids go to those schools?"

"Very nearly all," said his grandmother. "You had to be pretty far off the beaten path to avoid getting a forced

English education, but that's exactly where the Cooleys were—off the beaten path. They sent their children to illegal 'hedge schools.' My grandmother Cooley spoke Irish, Latin, and Greek, but very little English until she came to America.''

"Do you know any Irish, Grandma?''

"I think I may have known a bit as a child, but it wasn't really spoken at home. All I can recall now is a thing or two I can't repeat in polite company,'' Frances admitted. "Your mother would kill me if I taught any of it to you.''

"Did you teach her?''

"Your grandfather did, rest his soul, when she was only six years old. He thought it was the funniest thing on the Earth. I didn't speak to him for a whole day on account of it, and he thought that was the *second* funniest thing on the Earth.''

"We'll talk later,'' Peter stage-whispered to his grandmother.

"You're hopeless, the two of you,'' said Jackie.

"Well, I certainly hope so, dear,'' said Frances.

CHAPTER 5

Jackie sighed with relief when the bell rang at the end of her Friday film lab. "Class on Tuesday," she reminded her departing students. "Don't forget there'll be a tiny little test." A few of the students managed good-natured groans on their way out of the room. She had just finished showing them *The Best Years of Our Lives* and *All My Sons* as part of this semester's Film and Society class. They had seemed to enjoy these two very different looks at an America none of them had ever seen, and she anticipated a lot of lively discussion about them next week.

Last semester she'd managed to get the class through the Great Depression and the war, and now they were exploring the post-World-War-Two world as viewed through the film-maker's lens. Jackie would like to have been able to concentrate on the films more closely herself this morning, but the strange events of the previous day were still troubling her.

She hadn't been able to get that poor dead woman in the alley out of her mind, or her poor dog, either. A phone call to Tom had assured her the little terrier was doing well, though he seemed lonely. Joseph was spending extra time with him whenever he could be spared from other duties, and everything was being done to make him as happy as possible.

Jackie wished with all her heart the dog still had his own

24

mistress to make him happy, but fate hadn't been that kind to the little guy. It wasn't really her responsibility what happened to him, but she felt like she had taken something on when she had pulled him out from under a trash container and taken him to Tom Cusack. She felt a similar responsibility to his dead owner, though she couldn't say exactly why.

Now with her morning obligations finished and no office hours this afternoon, Jackie looked forward to having some of her questions answered. And she knew just the man to answer them, too—Cosmo Gordon, Palmer's Chief Medical Examiner. She snagged her coat and handbag from the coat rack near her desk and hurried out the door. If she sped just a tiny bit, she could make it from the Rodgers University campus to the City Morgue in time to grab Cosmo for lunch.

Jackie and Cosmo had become friends over the last few years, even though the mutual friend who had introduced them, Michael McGowan, was now effectively out of Jackie's life. A lot had changed in those years, including Jackie and Michael's relationship. They were now cautious friends rather than lovers.

But Jackie wasn't the only one whose life had changed. Cosmo's wife of nearly thirty years had filed for divorce the previous year, and poor Cosmo had seemed terribly lost for the first six months or so. He was beginning to get back on his feet now, though he had yet to start dating again. Jackie looked forward to spending some time in his company and not, she assured herself, just because she could almost certainly worm some details out of him about the Jane Doe case.

"Jackie! How's the little dog doing?"

Jackie had been walking up the steps to the Palmer City Morgue right next door to the Palmer Police Department when she heard someone calling out. She turned around to see Bernie Youngquist walking toward her, perfectly turned out without seeming to have worked at it in pleated chocolate trousers and a cream silk shirt under a wool suit jacket, and every shining golden hair in place.

"He's fine at last report," Jackie told her, trying to sound friendlier than she felt.

"I'm so glad," said Bernie. "The Medical Examiner's office should be publishing the results of the autopsy today, and we'll know whether or not he needs to stay under wraps, or whether he can start finding a new home." She smiled, flashing her perfect white teeth.

Jackie smiled back, hoping her insecurities weren't showing. She supposed she shouldn't mind that Bernie Youngquist was probably the best-looking woman in Palmer. Jackie had a steady boyfriend, so it wasn't like they were in competition for the available bachelors, but there it was. Towering over Bernie by a good five inches and not nearly so delicate-looking, Jackie felt sort of like a Rottweiler being shown next to a greyhound—sturdy, loyal, serviceable—but lacking somehow in the quality of ethereal grace.

"I'd like to go visit the little guy when I get off duty," said Bernie. "Could you give me the address of your friend's kennels?"

"Oh. Sure." Jackie rummaged around in her handbag and came up with one of Tom's cards. "It's on the east end of town, sort of out in the countryside," she told her.

"I'll find it on my map," said Bernie, tucking the card into her coat pocket. "I'm learning my way around Palmer slowly but surely. I'd still like to get together with you—are you free for lunch?"

"Actually, I was just on my way in to see Cosmo Gordon."

"Not official business, I hope."

"No, just a visit to an old friend. Maybe we can do lunch some other time?"

"Absolutely," said Bernie. "I'll be around for the foreseeable future. You take it easy, now."

"Thanks. You too." Jackie retreated through the big, brass-handled wooden doors of the morgue with a guilty flood of relief. It wasn't Bernie Youngquist's fault Jackie found her so damned intimidating. Jackie knew she should be a whole lot more mature about the whole thing—if she could manage that, she might just end up with a new friend into the bargain.

"But I'm not that mature, damn it!"

"Excuse me?" asked the young woman behind the reception desk.

"Sorry. I'm here to see Cosmo Gordon."

"I'll ring him," said the woman, eyeing Jackie with the sort of caution often reserved for those who speak to themselves in public places.

"He's going to be just a minute or two," said the receptionist after she had gotten through to Cosmo's office. She gestured toward the waiting area. "Have a seat."

When Cosmo came through the half-door between the public front area and the offices and examination rooms that made up most of the ancient morgue building, he smiled at the sight of her. "Hi, Jackie. Did you come here to take an old man to lunch?"

"Well, I didn't know I did when I walked in here, but I think it's probably the best idea I've had so far today. Where shall we go? Don't you like to eat at the Juniper Tavern?"

"Nah, it's Yuppie Hell over there these days—all ferns and bamboo and stuff." He shuddered visibly. "I hate to see a good bar die, but that one's good and dead. Let's bury it, and walk over to Suzette's."

"Suzette's? You're kidding me. Do real men eat crêpes?"

"All the time," he assured her. "My favorite's the one with the smoked salmon and goat cheese."

Jackie shook her head. "I learn something new every day," she sighed.

"You always will if you're paying attention," Cosmo assured her. "Shall we go?"

Suzette's was plain and homey despite its name. The floors gleamed with coats of wax, and copper nail heads in the hardwood sparkled in the glow of mini-spotlights from the heavy wooden beams overhead. Little wooden tables sported unmatched cotton tablecloths and napkins, with a dime-store vase of fresh flowers on each table.

Cosmo ordered the *Crêpe Saumon*, and Jackie decided to try the *Crêpe Champignon*, with three different kinds of mushrooms. While they waited for their lunch to arrive, they sipped Suzette's famous *Café Noir*, a house blend heavy on the French Roast. Jackie added lots of cream to hers, but she suspected you could still tar your roof with it in a pinch.

"You know, I can't help but notice you haven't tried pumping me for information about that dead woman you found in the alley the other day," said Cosmo after a few minutes of light conversation over coffee, a slight smile visible at the edges of his lips.

"Jackie found a body? Not exactly what I'd call news!" The voice came from around the other side of a corner, and the blonde head that followed it to peek at Jackie and Cosmo belonged to none other than Marcella Jacobs, ace reporter for the Palmer *Gazette*.

"Hi, Marcella," said Jackie, not entirely grateful for the untimely interruption. She had been looking forward to whatever information Cosmo might have decided to volunteer, and Marcella's presence seemed very likely to inhibit him.

"You eating alone, Marcella? Why don't you join us?" Cosmo offered. Evidently, Cosmo wasn't as inhibited by Marcella as Jackie had thought. Of course he was single now, and that had a way of giving a man a whole different outlook.

"I'd love to," said Marcella, and Jackie could swear she was actually batting her eyelashes at Cosmo. She rolled her own eyes toward the ceiling, but neither of them seemed to notice. Marcella retrieved her mug of coffee from her table and waved at the server to signal her change of venue.

"So Jackie found a body in an alley? Not exactly new, but it just might turn out to be news all the same. Tell me all the gory details," Marcella insisted, practically wriggling with anticipation.

"There's really nothing to tell . . ."

"A homeless Jane Doe . . ."

Jackie and Cosmo began to speak simultaneously, then stopped and looked at one another.

Marcella looked back and forth between the two of them, and seemed to decide that Palmer's Medical Examiner was a far better bet for juicy tidbits of information than her old friend Jackie.

"I know about the body, of course," she told him, dismissing her insider status with a practiced wave of her hand, "but no one told me Palmer's celebrated amateur detective was involved."

"I'm not involved!" Jackie protested. Never mind Marcella's "detective" crack—just the sort of thing that Jackie found irritating about her old school chum. "I just sort of stumbled across the body!"

"Oh, you're far too graceful to have stumbled over anything," Marcella objected. "You were probably looking for clues to some other murder, if I know you."

"Well, this one wasn't a murder," Cosmo informed her. "In fact, that's what I was getting ready to tell Jackie when you overheard us."

"Well, that's a relief," said Jackie. At least now they could drop all this talk about her checkered past where Palmer, Ohio murders were concerned. She had had enough of the whole subject to last her for the rest of her natural life.

"Not a murder, huh?" said Marcella, sounding more than a little disappointed. "Too bad. News around here has been so slow that the Save the Market campaign has made the front page three times this week. Of course I can't exactly complain about that, since they assigned me the story."

"Jackie's Jane Doe died of simple exposure in a trash container while falling-down drunk," said Cosmo. "Her blood alcohol count was through the ceiling. It looks like she crawled inside and passed out, and the rest is history. Sad, but not exactly front page news."

"But what about the dog?" Jackie asked.

"What about it?" Cosmo wanted to know.

"What dog?" asked Marcella.

"Jackie found a dog when she found the body," Cosmo informed Marcella. "I heard all about it from that new detective, Bernie Youngquist."

"It was sort of the other way around," said Jackie. "The dog was hiding under the dumpster. That's how I found the body. But I keep wondering one thing: if the woman crawled inside the dumpster, why did she leave her dog *outside*?"

"Who says it was her dog?" asked Marcella.

"No one, I guess," Jackie sighed. "Maybe that's the fatal flaw in my reasoning. Maybe it wasn't her dog at all."

"Well, it makes a better story if it is," Marcella assured them. "Where's the dog now?"

"Tom's boarding him," Jackie told her. "I guess now that the death has been declared accidental, he can be adopted. Maybe I can take out an ad in the *Gazette*."

"We can do better than that," said Marcella. "I'll go out to Tom's after lunch and get some pictures of him. I can get the editor to run a column in tomorrow's paper. He'll have more offers than a movie star."

Their orders arrived, and most of the rest of the meal was spent in small talk between Cosmo and Marcella, with Jackie taking the role of observer. She couldn't help noticing that Cosmo seemed unusually animated since Marcella sat down with them. Marcella, in her turn, appeared intently interested in everything Cosmo had to say, and they leaned into one another slightly as they talked.

Jackie observed their body language and wondered what, if anything, she should make of it. Was this a romance in the making she was watching unfold here? Cosmo was probably twenty years older than Marcella, which scarcely mattered to Jackie, but Marcella had always seemed to prefer them young, handsome, and flighty. Interesting, to say the least.

A copy of the Local News section of today's Palmer *Gazette* was peeking out of Marcella's blazer pocket, and Jackie pulled it out without Marcella even noticing. She smiled in satisfaction as she unfolded the paper. Maybe she had an illustrious career as a pickpocket somewhere in her future. She could always hope.

The feature story carried on the front page of the section carried Marcella's byline—no wonder she was carrying it around with her—and the headline: "A New Era for Palmer's Market District?" was suitably dramatic for a story of no interest to anyone more than five miles outside Palmer, Ohio. Jackie started to read the story, but was interrupted by Marcella.

"Pretty good stuff, huh?" Marcella pointed a lacquered nail at the paper in Jackie's hands. "It's the third of a five-part series I'm doing on the Farmers' and Growers' Market controversy."

"What controversy is that?" Jackie asked.

"What planet have you been living on, girl?" Marcella demanded. "It's the only thing people are talking about downtown."

"Cosmo?" Jackie held up the paper. "Am I the only one who's out of touch?"

"Oh, I guess I've heard it mentioned," he said, "but I can't say I've paid too much attention to it, as busy as I've been. I'm very sorry to say I haven't read Marcella's articles . . ."

"If you like, I'll have them sent over to your office, Cosmo."

"Why, thank you." Cosmo beamed at her briefly and went on. "Isn't it about someone proposing to tear down the old Farmers' and Growers' Market and build something else in its place?"

"That's right. The City owns Farmers' and Growers', and since they started pumping money into it, encouraging shopkeepers to come in, cleaning up the area. Well that whole old neighborhood between Fourth and Seventh avenues has really started to take off—new restaurants, shops—property values are soaring anywhere within a mile of F and G."

"So what's the problem?" Jackie asked her.

"Well, a lot of people on the City Council think that the area would grow even faster *without* the Market."

"But you just said the Market was the reason it grew in the first place."

"That's what the other half of the City Council says," replied Marcella. "That, and it's an historic part of Old Palmer that ought to be preserved for its own sake, not to mention the sake of the tourist dollars it's starting to bring in."

Jackie agreed with that. Her apartment was in one of the recently renovated areas of Palmer, not too far away from the old market building, and she rather liked the old places around there that had gotten a face-lift instead of being demolished out of hand. "I don't get it," she admitted. "If it's making money . . ."

"Maybe somebody thinks they can make even more money by tearing it down," Cosmo offered.

"You're absolutely right, Cosmo," said Marcella, as Cosmo blushed becomingly. "This picture"—she indicated an architect's concept drawing that was reproduced next to a picture of the newly refurbished Farmers' and Growers' Market—"shows what they think is going to make them that money."

Jackie looked at the picture of a seven-story glass-and-steel building—a modified ziggurat with hanging gardens on every level, surrounded by little rectangles of manicured turf, happy shoppers, and those perfect little trees that only architects, it seems, have ever laid eyes on.

"Shops on the first floor, offices on Two and Three, condos on Four through Seven, acres of underground parking. What do you think?"

"It's not a bad-looking building, I guess, but it doesn't really fit into the whole atmosphere of the Market District. This . . ." she looked at the signature on the drawing ". . . Jay Garnett person should have known better than to try to fit this building into that neighborhood. I think this whole plan is a serious mistake, and frankly I hope it goes up in flames." She handed the newspaper back to Marcella.

"Oh, I don't know," said Marcella, looking at the drawing. "Maybe Palmer could use a little modernizing. That old market building is getting pretty long in the tooth."

"So's the Lincoln Memorial, but no one's suggesting that Washington, D.C. demolish it in favor of a shopping mall," Jackie countered. "The Farmers' and Growers' Market is part of Palmer's history, Marcella. It's a beautiful old building full of interesting shops and restaurants that contribute a lot to the community, and whose owners probably couldn't afford the sky-high rents in your gleaming tower of yuppiedom there." She stabbed a finger at the picture.

"Well, don't bite my head off," Marcella objected, clutching the paper protectively to her chest. "Times change." She looked at Cosmo for support.

"I'm afraid I'm in Jackie's camp on this one," said Cosmo. "I remember when they still used to allow horses inside the Market building, not that there were that many of them around, even then. I think the Farmers' and Growers' is one thing the modernizers ought to leave the hell alone."

"Time alone will tell, I guess," said Marcella. "That and how much influence the Cockrills can bring to bear on the Council."

Jackie recognized the name of one of Palmer's oldest and wealthiest families. "What have they got to do with it?"

"The land the Market stands on originally belonged to the Garnett family, and the former Ada Garnett is Mrs. Felix Cockrill. Her parents deeded it to the City in 1896 as part of a trade for some other property. So it doesn't exactly belong to them, but they have a lot of influence on what goes on downtown. Between Felix and Ada, they own most of the rest of downtown Palmer."

"So I'd guess they want it preserved, right?"

"You'd be wrong," said Marcella. "They're the ones leading the fight to tear it down."

CHAPTER 6

With Marcella sitting at the table, Jackie hadn't got anything more out of Cosmo about poor, dead Jane Doe, but at least she could rest easy on the subject of murder. She looked at her watch as she left Suzette's and waved goodbye to Cosmo and Marcella, who were walking off together, their offices being only a couple of blocks apart.

Jackie started to walk off in the direction of her car, then stopped and turned as a thought occurred to her. "Cosmo!" she called.

Cosmo turned back around.

"What's going to happen to her?"

"Who?"

"You know—Jane Doe. What will happen if no one claims her?"

"Our policy is to hold on to the remains of unidentified individuals for thirty days. If no one steps forward to identify her in that time, she'll be buried at the county's expense in the county cemetery."

Jackie stood there thinking about this for a long moment.

"Does that answer your question?" Cosmo asked.

"Oh. Yes. Thanks, Cosmo."

"Don't mention it, Jackie. Thanks for lunch."

"My pleasure," she replied, but the two of them had already turned back. Marcella chatted animatedly to Cosmo as they walked away, and Cosmo seemed to have a new

spring in his step. Jackie decided it was going to be interesting, at the very least, to see how this new friendship
developed.

Peter wouldn't be home for two more hours, and she had
let Jake and Charlie out before she left for class this morning—she could afford a little time to herself. The Farmers'
and Growers' Market was only about seven blocks from
here, and despite some snow still clumped up in the shadier
spots of the sidewalks, it was a beautiful day. She decided
to walk.

Palmer's oldest and most familiar surviving landmark
had been erected just before the turn of the century to give
local farmers a place to sell their goods to the public, and
to give the public relief from the higher prices charged by
the retail markets.

From fruits and vegetables brought in from outlying
farms, items on sale at the Farmers' and Growers' Market
had expanded to feature fresh flowers, honey, preserves,
eggs, and other products. It soon became a busy and popular spot for locals to shop and meet friends, and the place
people tended to bring out-of-town visitors. Never been to
Palmer before? You've got to see the Market!

Over the years the Market had grown from a handful of
fruit and vegetable stalls into a huge building with lots of
tall windows, and rows of big sliding doors to allow horse-
drawn wagons and later, trucks to pull inside. It attracted
merchants of all kinds into a sort of old-time super-mall
where Palmer's citizens could shop for just about anything
they might need under one three-block-long roof.

As time went by and the neighborhood near the railroad
tracks began to tarnish a bit, the most successful and up-
wardly mobile sort of businesses had moved on to outlying
locations to follow the de-urbanizing population, and the
more modest businesses either failed and were replaced by
other modest businesses, or eked out a living in the slowly
deteriorating environment of downtown Palmer's Market
District.

A few years back, shortly before Jackie had left the stifling life of suburban Kingswood, Ohio and her marriage

to Cooper Walsh behind, things had begun to change for Palmer's oldest districts. With some matching funds from state and federal governments, the city had begun to make a real effort to revitalize some of the older neighborhoods.

Jackie's own apartment, formerly half of a small industrial building facing a wide, brick alleyway, had become a condo, and the alley itself had become what was now called Isabella Lane. Even the old movie palace between here and her apartment—the Sofia Cinema—had escaped the wrecking ball to emerge as a spruced-up sentimental favorite with Palmer's movie fans. Only the area immediately surrounding the Market itself, and the even seedier blocks across the railroad tracks, had yet to feel the influence of the revitalization of central Palmer.

"Save the Market! Join the campaign! Save the Market!" Jackie looked for the source of the voice and saw a pretty woman with a head of unruly red hair waving a sheaf of bright green flyers and handing them off to passersby.

"I'll take one of those," she said, reaching out her hand for a flyer. The red-haired woman smiled and handed her one. "Are you interested in joining our campaign to save Farmers' and Growers'?"

"I just might be," said Jackie. "I think it would be a crime if they tore this place down."

"You've got that right," said the red-haired woman. "We're having a meeting tonight if you'd like to attend. The time and place are on the flyer. Hope to see you there." She put a flyer into the hand of a man who ventured too close to escape it. "Save the Market!" she said, with real feeling.

Jackie scanned the flyer as she walked away. The words *Save the Market* appeared prominently in bold, black type, followed by several paragraphs of impassioned copy and a bulleted list of reasons why any reasonable person would agree that the Market needed saving. Well, Jackie agreed, anyhow. She folded the flyer and tucked it into her jacket pocket.

Jackie walked around the first level of the Farmers' and Growers' Market, dodging determined lunchtime shoppers and trying to imagine herself in the ground floor of a three-block-long mega-mall straddling a parking garage and carrying an apartment building on its back. She couldn't. The sights and sounds and smells of the old Market were too vivid, too real, for her to imagine it as anything else, especially anything so antiseptic. She couldn't smell horses, and that was probably for the best, but people still milled around the produce stands, picked over the day's offerings, and listened to the cries of dealers proclaiming the freshness of their wares, just as they had ninety years before.

She closed her eyes for a moment and envisioned what it must have been like in the old days, with horse-drawn wagons bringing in produce every morning before the sun was up. Someone jostled her and she lost her balance for a moment. She opened her eyes and took a step backwards.

"Ow! My foot!"

"Oh, gosh, I'm sorry!" Jackie turned around to see a tall, nice-looking man standing on one leg, cradling the foot she had stepped on in two large, long-fingered hands. "Did I break it?"

"I don't think so," said the man. "I guess it just surprised me. I'm afraid I was standing here with my eyes shut. Pretty dumb, huh?" People swirled around him as he stood there on one leg. A few of them stared.

The man gave her an embarrassed smile and put the foot down cautiously. "See? It's fine." Good humor enlivened his long, pleasant face.

"Well, I'm glad it's not broken, but I don't think I could agree that what you were doing was dumb," Jackie said. "The fact is I wouldn't have stepped on you in the first place if I hadn't been standing here with my eyes shut, too."

"You're kidding me!" he exclaimed. "Why?"

"You first," Jackie challenged.

"Okay. I was trying to imagine what it would be like if the Market weren't here anymore, and another building were put up in its place."

"Oh, you mean the ziggurat thing that was in the paper,"

said Jackie, nodding. "You don't have to imagine too hard—it'd be a tragedy."

"Do you really think so?" the man asked, sounding genuinely interested in the answer.

"Well, since you asked, yes," Jackie told him. "I mean, the Market is an important part of Palmer, don't you think? A big piece of living history going back almost a hundred years. It'd be a shame to lose that, wouldn't it? Well, I think so, anyhow.

"And take a look at this neighborhood while you're at it," she went on. "Most of it dates from around the same time as this building. You try to stick that seven-story glass monstrosity into this area, it'll stand out like a sore thumb. So there you have one tragedy and one example of bad taste."

She stopped ranting for a moment and looked at the man, who was regarding her with utter seriousness, nodding his head. "I'm terribly sorry," she said. "Here I am rambling on about something you probably don't even care about, and I haven't even introduced myself." She held out her hand. "I'm Jackie Walsh."

The man shook her hand. "Well, I actually do care, Ms. Walsh," he said with a good-natured smile. "I'm Jay Garnett. I designed the, uh, seven-story glass monstrosity."

Jackie groaned. "I think this is where I die of embarrassment," she said.

"Oh, don't worry about it," Jay Garnett reassured her with a wave of his hand. "I'm used to people not liking Market Place. I don't like it that much myself, but Felix insisted I design it, then proceeded to reject every single concept I offered him that actually made an effort to harmonize with the neighborhood. It was a real nightmare." He looked around at his surroundings and shook his head. "In fact, it's been the worst thing that's ever happened to me, if you want to know the truth."

"Well, I'm sorry to hear that, Mr. Garnett."

"Jay. Please."

"You work for Felix Cockrill, Jay?"

"Worse. He's my brother-in-law."

"Well, I'm sorry to hear it. I hope things improve for you soon."

Jay Garnett sighed. "It could happen. My sister could leave Felix for the pool man, or Felix could have a sudden loss of memory that causes him to abandon the Market Place project—not the likeliest possibility—or I could get hit by a crosstown bus." His dark eyes twinkled, but there was an unmistakable air of genuine sadness to his words.

"It's none of my business of course," Jackie began, then hesitated.

"Then that probably makes it more interesting," said Jay. "What's none of your business?"

Jackie wondered why she was discussing something so personal with a man she'd only just stepped on a minute before, but there was something very warm and open about Jay Garnett, and it made her approach him with an equal openness. "This is so crass I wish I'd never brought it up," Jackie told him, "but if you're Ada Garnett's brother, why aren't you rich?"

"You know, that's the question I always used to ask my father's lawyers," said Jay, "but the fact is he left everything but an old house on Cedar Street to Ada. I don't even know where he got the house—knowing Dad, he probably put a little old couple out on the street." He smiled when he said that, but Jackie could tell he wasn't really joking.

"Anyhow the house is mine now, and everything else is my sister's. Maybe I didn't show enough of the Garnett killer instinct to make him think he ought to trust me with any of his money."

"Well, I hope your foot recovers anyhow," Jackie offered.

Jay lifted the foot and moved it around. "One hundred percent cured," he pronounced. "Nice meeting you, Jackie. Maybe we'll bump into one another again sometime. But next time I get to step on your foot."

"It's a deal," said Jackie, laughing.

Jay Garnett gave her a wave and walked back into the crowd of shoppers.

No wonder the Market Place building didn't work, she

thought. Even the architect didn't believe in it. Jackie thought it was nearly as much of a shame for a nice guy like Jay Garnett to have to carry the proposed Market Place building around his neck like some kind of architectural albatross as it was for Palmer to have to risk having it built in the first place.

The south entrance to Farmers' and Growers' was only half a block from the scene of Jane Doe's death, and Jackie realized as she neared it that a part of her had known since she left Suzette's with Cosmo and Marcella that this was where she was really headed. As she approached the alleyway from its north end, she saw a shabbily dressed man walking stooped over among the trash bins, and heard him whistle and snap his fingers.

"Arlo!" the man called. "Where are you, Arlo? Come on out, boy." He caught sight of Jackie standing on the sidewalk a few feet away. "Don't suppose you've seen a little dog around here—tan and white, about so big?" he asked her. "He's got kind of scruffy fur and a little brown collar."

"Is it your dog?" Jackie inquired. She walked a few steps towards him, slowly.

The man regarded Jackie with a guarded expression. He had a broad, flat face ringed by tight brown and gray curls and a graying beard, and dominated by pale blue eyes that were a little bloodshot. His body was large and powerful under the faded clothing. He looked like a man accustomed to getting his way through force of will, or maybe his fists. The nose had been broken more than once, she guessed.

"Belonged to a friend," he said shortly. "I'm afraid the little guy must've froze to death the other night when it snowed." A tear worked its way out of one eye and ran down his cheek. "Can't even afford to bury my friend—I thought the least I could do is take care of her dog, if I could find it. Doesn't look like I will, though." He made a helpless gesture at the empty alley, and shook his head sadly.

Jackie considered whether or not to volunteer information to this stranger, but then the dead woman had been a stranger to her, too, and that hadn't stopped her from assuming the role of protector to her dog.

"I know where he is," she began. "Uh, Arlo? Is that his name? I know where Arlo is. I found him out here yesterday morning." She decided to omit the fact that she had also found the man's dead friend. "A friend of mine is caring for him."

"Really?". The man's face broke into a wide smile. "That's great news. He's got a place to stay out of the cold?"

Jackie nodded. "A temporary place, anyhow. So you were a friend of . . . the woman who died here?"

"Yeah, Rosie 'n' me went back a ways. She helped me learn my way around when I came here a couple of years back. She was a good one, that Rosie. Damned if I know how come she died like that."

"From what I hear, she'd been drinking and fell asleep. It got really cold that night . . ."

The big man cocked his head at Jackie. After a moment he nodded. "Yeah, it was damned cold that night, but Rosie wasn't drinking." He spoke with a certainty that made Jackie curious about his meaning.

"How can you be so sure?" she asked him.

"'Cause Rosie didn't drink," the man told her, looking steadily into her eyes. "Not a drop. She was allergic to booze."

CHAPTER 7

Jackie absorbed this bit of information slowly, letting it sink in and bring with it the realization that just possibly her discovery of the body in the alley yesterday morning was no longer mercifully free of the shadow of murder.

"You're absolutely sure she wouldn't have drunk any alcohol that night?" she asked, trying to keep her voice steady.

"Yeah, I'm sure. Who the hell are you to be asking?" The man had pulled himself up into a stance of quiet aggression, eyes narrowed and fists clenched. He took a step towards her.

"I'm sorry," Jackie said. "I didn't mean to offend you." She felt more defeated than afraid, she realized, as if the knowledge of murder and her involvement in it—however slight—was a stronger force than the threat posed by some guy who looked like an ex-boxer, and who appeared ready to stop her clock if she insulted his dead friend one more time. "I'm the one who found your friend's body."

The man just looked at Jackie for a long moment, then his body seemed to relax as he reached out a hand. "Name's Eugene," he told her. "Eugene Seybold. Thanks for taking care of Arlo—a guy needs all the friends he can get in this world, even if he happens to be a dog." He chuckled. "Or maybe especially if he's a dog. But don't you let them try to tell you Rosie Canty died 'cause she was drunk, 'cause that never happened.''

Jackie shook his hand. "I'm Jackie Walsh," she said. "I'm terribly sorry about your friend. I'm sure the police . . .''

"The police don't care," said Eugene Seybold, shaking his head. "Maybe they'd get all concerned if it was somebody like you that died, but what's it to them if some poor woman with no place to go dies in a dumpster? How many times you reckon that happens in this country on any cold night?''

Jackie opened her mouth to object, but realized she couldn't actually promise Eugene Seybold that there would be an investigation. The Medical Examiner's Office had already chalked up the woman's death to a tragic accident brought on by alcoholism, and without some compelling new evidence even she knew that the Palmer Police Department wasn't likely to get involved.

"I care," was all she could say. "I have friends on the police force." Well, she had Evan Stillman, and maybe he wasn't exactly a friend, but he'd do in a pinch. "I'll tell the police what you said about Rosie never drinking. Maybe they'll investigate further.''

"Thanks, Mrs. Walsh. Miss Walsh?''

"Ms. Or just Jackie is fine.''

"Thanks, Jackie, but they'd be more inclined to investigate if old Felix Cockrill stubbed his big toe than if you could show them someone murdered Rosie Canty. I'm sorry if I sound cynical, but I've been on the street off and on for years, and this isn't the first time something like this has happened, and you can bet it won't be the last.''

He turned and walked away from her down the alley, his head bent low. Jackie watched him go almost to the sidewalk at Indiana Street before he stopped and turned back around. "You say hi to Arlo for me, okay?" He raised a hand.

Jackie returned his wave. "I will," she promised him.

Jackie pulled her coat around her as she negotiated the remaining heaps of snow still piled here and there on the

shady side of Fourth Avenue. She had never felt so lucky
to have a coat, or a car to be going to, or a home to drive
to in that car, and she wondered how she had gone this
long taking it all for granted.

She unlocked the Blazer and drove home deep in
thought, grateful that she could summon enough presence
of mind to remain marginally alert in traffic. Eugene Seybold's words kept coming back to her. *Don't let them try
to tell you Rosie died 'cause she was drunk,* he'd said, but
that was exactly what the official report had claimed. Who
was likelier to be right about a thing like this—the City's
Medical Examiner, or a shabby man with no home to go
to tonight who had known the dead woman well? She
wished she knew.

Her watch told her she could go by and visit Tom at the
kennels and still be home not long after Peter got home
from school. He was still working on his family history
project, and his grandmother had him checking out genealogy websites on the internet. That would keep him busy
and amused for a while, she figured.

Jackie supposed she would have to make sure he was
keeping up with his other homework, too, before he went
netsurfing in cyberspace until bedtime and beyond, but she
couldn't deny it was fun seeing him get such a kick out of
schoolwork. Pity it had taken a fugitive from justice hiding
out in the branches of the family tree to ignite his enthusiasm, but she supposed every family had its black sheep.

She pulled her car up in the long, curving front driveway
that led from the two-lane Springfield Highway to Cusack
Kennels. A small white compact was parked at the head of
the drive, behind Tom's old Cherokee, and Jackie pulled
up as far from it as possible so its owner wouldn't have a
problem getting out.

As she pulled the key from the ignition she saw Bernie
Youngquist come walking out of the Kennel building, wave
to someone behind her, and get into the little white car. She
knew she probably ought to try to get Bernie's attention,
be friendly, but somehow she couldn't bring herself to

make the effort. She stayed behind the wheel and watched as the little car backed skillfully down the drive and turned out onto the two-lane highway.

"Jackie?" She turned at the sound of Tom's voice. "Why are you sitting in your car? Come on out of there and give me a kiss."

Jackie hadn't even realized she'd been sitting there without moving since Bernie had appeared. She shook her head, laughing at herself. "I'm weirding out, as Peter would say," she told Tom. "And that kiss sounds like the best idea you've ever had." She climbed down out of the car and into Tom's arms.

"Actually, the best idea I ever had was for us to move in together," said Tom into her neck. "Or maybe it was the one about getting married . . ."

"Shut up and kiss me," she said.

He did. Then he told Joseph to answer the phone for an hour.

"So Bernie says your Jane Doe died of exposure, and the Police Department has no further interest in our little friend in the kennel." They were sitting in Tom's kitchen, drinking coffee and holding hands across the tiny Formica-topped table Tom had bought from an antiques dealer in Farmers' & Growers'. Tom had mentioned that Bernie had come to visit the dog and ended up staying quite a while.

"Yeah, that's what they say," said Jackie.

"What is that I hear in your voice, Jacqueline Shannon Costello?" said Tom, imitating Jackie's mother to perfection. "Could it be doubt? Do you possibly have a better opinion?"

Jackie laughed at his Frances Costello impression. "I guess not," she said, "and I sure don't have any facts, but I do have information, of a sort."

"Do tell." Tom reached for the coffee pot and filled up her cup without letting go of her hand.

"The dog's name is Arlo," Jackie began, "and his owner's name was Rosie. Rosie Canty."

"That's good to know, but it doesn't explain all those

thoughts I can see swirling around behind those beautiful dark eyes of yours, my darling girl. There's something else, isn't there? Out with it, my love. If you can't tell me what you're thinking, you can't tell anybody.''

Jackie sighed. Tom was right, of course. She had never felt safer opening up to anyone than she felt with him, but her curiosity about this case and her unwillingness to let it go were different from the usual confidences she shared so willingly. "The other thing is that the autopsy revealed a lot of alcohol in her bloodstream, but I met a friend of hers today and he told me she never drank.''

"Well, it was pretty cold out that night," Tom said. "Sometimes people drink to feel warm, even though it's an illusion.''

"He told me she was allergic," said Jackie. "He was very emphatic about it. He seemed to know her pretty well.''

"What can I say?" Tom shrugged his shoulders. "Maybe he was wrong.''

Jackie nodded. "Someone was wrong.''

Tom shook his head. "Oh, no. Tell me you're not thinking about digging into this." He was laughing, but uneasily.

"Not exactly. But I'd like to get Cosmo to check it out. Maybe there was a mistake about the blood alcohol level. I'm not talking about foul play or anything—she could still have died of exposure, couldn't she?''

"Of course she could. Almost certainly," Tom agreed, perhaps too eagerly.

"And that doesn't necessarily mean anyone helped her along, does it?''

"Almost certainly not.''

"But it was you who wondered why she would have crawled into the trash bin to keep warm and left her dog outside.''

"That's why we weren't sure it was her dog," Tom re- called.

"Exactly. But the man I met downtown today—Eugene Seybold—said it *was* her dog. He described him perfectly. So I guess we're back to square one, aren't we?''

"Unless her friend was wrong about her drinking, and she was just so drunk she forgot to bring the dog into the bin with her."

Jackie shook her head. "It just doesn't seem to work. Cosmo's theory can't be made to fit the facts unless someone who knew Rosie is mistaken about something so important as her being allergic to alcohol."

"You're assuming this Eugene guy was telling you the truth. Maybe he didn't want to admit his friend was an alcoholic. That's understandable, isn't it? He might have thought you'd judge her for it."

"I guess it could be, but I don't know." She looked over at Tom. "I guess he could have been saying it so I wouldn't think badly of her. I guess that could be it." Her words seemed to take away some of the worry in Tom's eyes, and Jackie was glad she had said them, even though she didn't actually believe them.

CHAPTER 8

The meeting of the Save the Market Campaign was being held in A Readers' Market, a cozy, crowded bookstore with lots of nooks and crannies and easy chairs for sitting and reading, located on the Market's upper level between a rubber stamp store and a health food co-op. Gillian Zane, the redheaded woman Jackie had seen passing out campaign flyers earlier in the day, was the owner of the bookstore and the head of the Save the Market campaign.

Gillian had provided a wide variety of food and drinks, and Jackie was glad she had decided to bring her mother along so there wouldn't be any problems with pesky leftovers. Frances had gone straight for the refreshments as soon as they had hung their coats on the coat tree near the door, and having sampled widely, she was now prepared to give the spread a rave review.

"The shortbread biscuits are simply to die for, Jacqueline," Frances assured her around a mouthful of the pastry in question. Several more adorned her plate. Jackie wondered, not for the first time, how her mother stayed so slim.

"When I think how much butter must be in each one," Jackie commented, eyeing the biscuits, "it gives the expression 'to die for' a whole new meaning. If it's all right with you, Mother, I think I'll just munch one of these carrot sticks instead."

She looked around at her surroundings, and at the small

but apparently sincerely concerned bunch who had gathered tonight to hear Gillian Zane lay out the problem and suggest solutions that might result in saving the Market from the wrecker's ball. Or more likely, Jackie supposed, these days they'd probably just use dynamite.

Most of the assembled were merchants renting space in Farmers' & Growers', but she saw a few other familiar faces, and trying discreetly to sneak a peek at everyone's handwritten name tags, Jackie recognized the names of several celebrities and prominent citizens of Palmer, including a number of wealthy downtown business owners, and the President of Palmer Savings and Loan, where she banked.

One golden head was recognizable clear across the room without the necessity for reading the little adhesive name tag—Marcella Jacobs, doubtless here to gather local color, human interest, and hard intelligence for the next article of her Market Place series in the Palmer *Gazette*. She was pulling on the arm of a handsome young man with long black hair who was wearing a black leather jacket and was loaded down with what looked like several hundred pounds of camera equipment, as she hurried across the room to Jackie.

"I see you were serious about not liking the Market Place proposal," said Marcella. "I never expected to see you here tonight."

"Well, I hadn't realized the extent of it when we talked at lunch," said Jackie, "but yes, I am serious." She extended a hand to the young man. "I don't think we've met."

"This is Leo McTaggart, a freelance photographer on assignment to me for the Market Place series," Marcella informed her. "Leo, meet Jackie Walsh, an old friend of mine. So how would you like your picture in tomorrow's paper?"

"Hi, Leo," said Jackie. "Save your film."

"Hi," said Leo. "How's the eats?" He pointed a slender finger at Jackie's plate of raw vegetables. "Marcella hasn't let me off my leash long enough to graze yet."

"You're not here to feed your face, Leo—you're here

to get the pictures I need,'' Marcella said without a trace of humor.

''Well, I hope we don't find your emaciated body in a corner of the bookstore later,'' said Jackie. Or if someone does find it, she thought to herself, I sure hope it's not me. ''Would you like some raw vegetables?'' She held out her plate.

''Ooh, Leo, look! It's Blair Brotherton. You know, Brotherton's?'' Marcella referred to Palmer's largest and classiest department store. ''Looks like he's finally decided which side of the Market Place issue he's on. Ooh! And Marianne Chung, Palmer's favorite T.V. chef! This is getting hot!''

Leo's hand was abruptly jerked out of reach of Jackie's plate, just as he was closing in on a cherry tomato, and he and Marcella disappeared into the crowd. A moment later Jackie saw a flash. Marcella had got her man. Or woman. Whatever.

''Oh, you did come! Welcome, uh, Jackie.'' Gillian Zane read the name Jackie had printed onto her name tag with a permanent marker.

''I did, but I'm surprised you recognized me,'' said Jackie. ''You must have passed out hundreds of those flyers today.''

''I did,'' Gillian agreed, ''but most of the people didn't really want them.''

Gillian noticed Frances, who was standing near Jackie with a plate heaped with shortbread and mini-tarts. ''Hi, I'm Gillian, but I guess you know that already.'' She gestured apologetically at her name tag. ''Don't you hate these things? But they've become a habit at this sort of gathering.''

''We put them on, and then we keep on introducing ourselves anyway,'' Frances agreed. ''I'm Frances Costello. I'm also Jackie's mother, but I'm sure you won't hold that against me.''

''I'm very pleased to meet you, Frances.'' She did look pleased, actually, Jackie noted with some pleasure of her own. So many people said those words with their mouths while the rest of their faces betrayed the fact that they didn't actually give a good damn if they never saw you again. It was refreshing, as always, to encounter sincerity.

"I love to see faces that I don't recognize from the Farmers' and Growers' Merchants Association meetings," Gillian was saying to Frances. "It's really heartening to know people care about the Market, and that we can get people here to hear about the issues. Other than the ones who are directly affected, that is."

"Yes, I've already noticed a few pretty important people who might be able to influence the City Council on the issue," said Jackie. Marcella had noticed them all, too, she knew, and no doubt she had the pictures to prove it.

"Oh, you don't know the half of it," Gillian said confidentially. "We even have friends in the enemy camp. Come on over here and I'll introduce you."

Jackie and Frances followed Gillian across the crowded room to where two women—one perhaps a couple of years older than Jackie, the other barely out of her teens—stood holding paper cups of pink fruit punch and plates of Gillian's finger food. "Jackie Walsh, Frances Costello, I'd like you to meet Emma Cockrill and her sister Eden Cockrill."

"Cockrill?" Jackie couldn't stop the name from slipping out in her astonishment. "Uh, no relation, right?"

The older woman, whose name tag proclaimed her to be Emma, said nothing, but kept looking back and forth between Jackie and the floor. She seemed painfully shy. The younger one—Eden—smiled broadly. "On the contrary, Ms. Walsh. We're Felix Cockrill's daughters, but that doesn't mean we have to agree with him about the wisdom of tearing down Farmers' and Growers'." She was a very pretty young woman, with clear blue eyes and a shade of light brown hair almost identical to her sister's, but worn long and straight in contrast to her sister's rather severe style.

"We don't agree with Father on many things," said Emma, trying a smile and abandoning it in a split second. "Of course this is the first time we've done something so public about it.'' Her voice had diminished to almost a whisper by the end of her speech.

"Well, I'm very happy to meet you both,'' said Jackie.

"Pleased,'' said Frances. They shook hands all around.

Emma Cockrill glanced around at the dozens of people crowded into the little bookstore, seeming ready to shrink in fear at the slightest threat. Her left hand picked nervously at a neat gauze bandage wrapped around her right wrist. A similar one graced her left ankle.

"Emma had a run-in with a ferocious raspberry cane in the garden the other day,'' Eden joked, noticing the direction of Jackie's gaze. "She's an intrepid gardener, but it's not without its risks, as you can see.''

Emma seemed flustered at her younger sister's praise. "It's just a scratch,'' she said, making a dismissive gesture with the unbandaged hand. Her eyes still took in the room nervously.

"Don't you teach Film classes at Rodgers?'' Eden inquired.

"That's me,'' said Jackie. "Are you a student there, by any chance?''

Eden nodded. "Biology. I'm going to Veterinary School after I graduate.''

"Not if Father has anything to say about it,'' Emma murmured, almost to herself.

"I don't think I believe what I'm seeing!'' exclaimed a voice from behind Jackie. She didn't need to turn around to know it was Marcella, and it wasn't hard to figure out the reason for her surprise, especially when a camera's flash blinded her a moment later as Leo McTaggart recorded the moment for posterity.

"Well, the fat's in the fire now, Em,'' said Eden Cockrill. She didn't seem particularly upset by the fact, however.

"Father won't be at all happy about it,'' her sister said with a sigh. "I wish I hadn't let you talk me into coming tonight.''

"Forget the Local News section,'' Marcella whispered into Jackie's ear. "These ladies should land me the front page of the Sunday edition!''

"Marcella, I'd like you to meet Emma Cockrill and Eden Cockrill, as if you didn't already know exactly whose privacy you were invading."

"Oh, come on, Jackie—this is a public meeting. I'm not invading anything." Marcella turned to the two women. "I don't suppose either of you ladies would like to give me a brief statement to go along with this great photograph?"

"And speaking of great photographs," said Jackie, trying to shift the subject just a bit, "this is Leo McTaggart."

"How do you do?" said Leo. "Sorry about the intrusion," he said to Eden. "I can't make a living photographing animals and old buildings, so I sometimes have to take jobs like this. Doesn't mean I have to like it, though."

"You like old buildings, too?" Eden graced him with a lovely smile.

"As a matter of fact," Leo told her, "I've taken hundreds of shots of Farmers' and Growers' alone. I have a whole portfolio of them I've been sending around, trying to get them published."

"I'd love to see them sometime," Eden told him. Leo looked intensely happy to hear it.

"You know, Leo," Jackie informed him, "Rodgers University Press is looking for books about Palmer and environs for their publishing program. You should talk to a guy named Morgan Jones."

Leo beamed. "Thanks for the tip, Jackie."

"Any time."

"Leo!" Marcella was clearly not happy with her photographer's behavior.

Leo shrugged and moved just a little closer to Eden Cockrill.

"Well, my job is the news," Marcella told them, "and you can bet there's never going to be any shortage of it around my old friend Jackie." She clapped a hand onto Jackie's shoulder.

"That'll be enough of that," Jackie warned, but Marcella was oblivious, as usual.

"Why, did you know it was Jackie who discovered that poor woman's body only a couple of blocks from here just the other morning?'' Marcella inquired. ''And she rescued the woman's dog, too. And her boyfriend's boarding the little fellow in his kennel over on Springfield Road. Isn't that just the greatest? I got a great human-interest piece out of it to run in tomorrow's paper with a follow-up to the story about the unidentified dead woman.'' She looked terribly pleased with herself. ''Leo here got a prize-winning shot of the dog.''

''You found a dead body?'' Emma's face had gone completely white.

''You rescued a dog?'' Eden seemed genuinely interested.

''My daughter's always rescuing something or someone,'' Frances assured them. ''When she's not busy solving crimes, that is.''

''Mother . . .'' Jackie muttered. For once Frances seemed to get the hint.

''Evidently there's no crime involved. Now that they think the death was an accident, the police won't have any further interest in poor Arlo, and Tom will be looking for a good home for him.''

''Think?'' Marcella snorted. ''The report seemed pretty definite to me. Don't tell me you're on to something, Jackie.''

''No. Absolutely not. The case is closed. In fact, there never was a case in the first place. So there was no need for the police to ever be interested in the poor woman's dog in the second place.''

''The police were going to interview the dog?'' Gillian asked.

''They were pretty sure it was a witness to whatever happened,'' Jackie explained. ''If someone had killed the woman, the dog might have been able to identify the killer.''

Gillian turned to greet two people who were coming to join the group. ''George! Laura! Now that you two are here we can get started!''

''Not until I've had some of those tarts,'' said the tall, muscular black man whose name tag read George Venable.

He eyed Frances' plate of goodies with hungry eyes.

"I'll show you where I got 'em," Frances offered, and the two of them headed for the food table, chatting amiably.

"Well, let me introduce you to Laura Santillo before she develops a craving for the little meatballs," said Gillian.

"Never happen, Gill—I'm a hopeless vegetarian." The dark-haired woman smiled at Jackie. "Hi, I'm Laura. You're Jackie. Thank God for name tags, huh?"

"Simplifies everything. Hi."

"So are those carrot sticks the veggie option tonight?"

"No, there's lots of goodies over there for stalkers of the savage vegetable. Shall we go and join the other grazers?"

"Let's. Gill, give us a few minutes to chow, and we'll get this meeting started, okay?"

"It's a deal. I'll go set up the easel while you get your food."

"So are you a Farmers' and Growers' merchant, too?" Jackie asked Laura.

"Nope. I run the Women's Shelter over on South Iowa Street. We provide meals and beds and counseling and other services for homeless women."

"Are there a lot of homeless women in Palmer?" Jackie asked her. She had to admit the subject had been much on her mind of late.

"Well, the problem's pretty severe everywhere," said Laura. "I don't really think it's any worse in Palmer than anywhere else in the Midwest, but that's bad enough."

"Are most of these women alcoholics?" Jackie wondered.

"We see a little bit of everything," Laura told her. "We get a lot of women escaping abusive relationships, coming in with kids and needing a place to stay until they get a job or a ticket out of town. A lot of our clients are just temporarily down on their luck and don't have a family to provide emergency support."

She picked up a plate and began scanning the food table for suitable snacks. "Of course there are quite a few permanently homeless women in the city, too, to answer your second question. Most of them are drug abusers of one kind or another. And I guess the answer to your first question is that there are enough homeless women that we don't always have beds for them all.''

She speared a mushroom mini-quiche with a plastic fork and placed it on her plate. "George has a few beds for women at All Saints, but they're almost always taken, too. When they're not, he takes in my overflow. I'd be lost without George, and so would a lot of other people in this town.''

Jackie looked over to where her mother and George Venable were deep in conversation. "It must seem pretty hopeless sometimes," she observed. "I mean, you help people, but they're immediately replaced by more people that need help. It never ends, does it?''

"It ends for some of them," said Laura. "One of our permanently homeless women died of exposure the other night when it got so cold. Maybe you read about it in the paper.''

I can go you one better than that, Jackie thought, but decided not to bring up her involvement in the matter. Instead, she nodded and tried to think of something nonrevealing to say. "That was sad," was all she could come up with.

"That's for sure," Laura replied. She ate the turnover and took another. "I was out of beds that night, but I'd have made a place on the floor for Rosie, and her dog, too.'' She frowned. "And she knew that—it wouldn't have been the first time, either.

"There's been a lot of harassment of the homeless in this neighborhood lately," Laura went on, "more than just the usual opportunistic mugging. I mean real scary stuff. So far it's been directed at men only, but it's not the kind of thing you want to take chances with, and I've been telling the women every day how important it is to get off the streets at night. I can't imagine what could have possessed Rosie to spend the night out of doors.''

"The Medical Examiner said she was drunk at the time,''

Jackie offered. "Maybe that's why she ended up in the alley."

Laura stared at her. "I don't remember reading that in the paper," she said.

"It might not have been in the paper," Jackie confessed. "I have sort of an inside source, you might say."

Laura nodded. "Well, your inside source is way off, Jackie. A lot of homeless people have a problem with alcohol, but not Rosie. Her problem was she was just too emotionally disturbed to be able to hold down a job, or to deal with the world on a day-to-day basis. As a matter of fact, as far as I know she wouldn't touch the stuff for any reason. She said it gave her a raging headache."

CHAPTER 9

Jackie really hated the feeling that came and sat in the pit of her stomach at Laura's mention of Rosie Canty's aversion to alcohol. After talking to Tom this afternoon she had been able to rest a little easier about the whole thing. She had almost been able to convince herself that Eugene Seybold had told her something less than the absolute truth about his friend for whatever reasons he may have had.

It was harder to disbelieve his claim, however, when it came to her unasked, and from a seemingly unbiased source. So what the hell was going on? If Rosie Canty never took a drink, why was there enough alcohol in her blood when she died to make her "falling-down drunk," as Cosmo had stated? What could have induced her to drink if she didn't drink normally, and if she knew it would make her ill?

And what force in heaven or earth could have made her crawl into a trash bin after a snowstorm on a freezing cold night, leaving her dog outside in the snow, when she knew she had a place to stay only a few blocks away, where it was warm and dry?

"Okay, the meeting's about to get under way!" Gillian Zane called from the front of the bookstore, where she had set up a giant paper pad on an easel to illustrate her talk on the evils of Market Place and the necessity of preserving

Farmers' & Growers'. People began to migrate to that part of the room.

Jackie found a place to stand and watch Gillian, but many of the details of the presentation were lost on her. Her mind kept leaving the present discussion and going over and over the bare facts and strange suppositions of what she was coming to think of, in spite of her better judgment, as yet another murder case.

From what Jackie was able to gather from trying hard to pay attention, Gillian was speaking about the importance of preserving downtown Palmer history in general and Farmers' & Growers' Market in particular. Her plan was to form a Market Association, made up of Market merchants, local businesspeople, and interested citizens, to push for the creation of a historic district to protect Farmers' & Growers' and other historic buildings in the old neighborhood.

The district, as Gillian envisioned it, would be administered by a commission of Palmer citizens, and would be used to make Palmer more attractive to visitors and tourists without sacrificing the city's unique history and character. She wanted to propose the idea at this coming Tuesday's City Council meeting, and she had provided a sign-up sheet so that anyone interested could add their names to the list.

After Gillian was through telling about the Market Historic District, George Venable and Laura Santillo got up and talked about the public rest stop they planned to open on the ground floor of the old Central Hotel on Terminal Avenue, just across the railroad tracks from Farmers' & Growers'.

The hotel already housed a few dozen pensioners who couldn't afford the rent on a house or apartment, and because it had been a busy downtown meeting place in its salad days thirty or forty years ago, there were lots of extra toilet facilities on the ground floor, as well as a large meeting room that was presently being used for storage.

Under George and Laura's plan, homeless people could use the ground floor of the hotel to bathe, shave, and do laundry, making it easier for them to look for work. The plan would look for some funding from the city, but also

depend heavily on donations from downtown businesses
and various Palmer corporations. It was important, they emphasized, that when the Historic District was formed, Palmer's least fortunate not be overlooked.

George and Laura had come armed with lots of facts and
figures and floor plans to illustrate their part of the plan,
but the details were lost on Jackie in her distracted state of
mind. She did get the impression that there was a lot of
opposition to the rest stop idea from certain quarters in the
city, and that among the loudest dissenters were prominent
Palmer citizens Felix and Ada Cockrill.

"I swear, Jacqueline Shannon Costello, you've been staring
at the wall for the past hour. The meeting's over, and we're
practically the last people here. Don't you think we ought
to pay our respects to Gillian and get our tails home?"

"Huh?" Jackie shook herself out of her uncomfortable
reverie. "Oh, of course, Mother. Let's find her and say
good night."

They found Gillian at the food table, stuffing a trash bag
with paper plates and napkins. Jackie picked up another bag
from a pile on the floor and busied herself finding trash
where people had left it, usually not anywhere near one of
the containers provided. "Can we help with the vacuum-
ing?" Jackie asked.

"No, I'm going to do that in the morning before I open
up," Gillian said. "Right now I just want to go home and
collapse. Hey, thank you for coming, both of you. We're
going to need some support at the City Council meeting on
Tuesday night, too, when we propose the Market Historic
District. That is, if you're interested." She tied off both the
plastic bags and picked up her keys from the counter.
"There's a sign-up sheet on the counter here, if you are."

"I guess we could manage to attend the Council meeting,
couldn't we, Jacqueline?"

"Oh. Sure," said Jackie. "We'll be there. Strength in
numbers." She picked up a pen and added her name to the
list.

"You bet there is," said Gillian. She looked over the

list. "Look—even Marcella's photographer friend signed up. I'd be willing to bet she's not particularly happy about that."

"Marcella isn't exactly in favor of preserving the Market," Jackie admitted, "but her reaction to Leo's joining the Association will be ecstatic next to Felix Cockrill's when he sees his daughters' names and faces in Sunday's paper. I definitely wouldn't want to be there when he finds out."

"Me neither," Gillian admitted. "Have you ever met Felix Cockrill?"

Jackie and Frances shook their heads.

"A frightening man." She held open the doors that led out into the upper-level hallway of the Market. Jackie and Frances stepped through, and Gillian locked the doors behind them.

The Market was long closed, and the hallway was dark except for the moonlight that came in through the row of high windows above the stores. Jackie saw a tall and somehow familiar figure step out of the shadows near a supporting pillar.

"Gill, I need to talk to you," the man said. It was Jay Garnett, the architect she'd met in the Market this afternoon. He seemed not to notice either Jackie or Frances, so intent was he on Gillian.

"I've said everything I have to say to you, Jay," Gillian replied, and though Jackie couldn't see her face, she could clearly hear the strain in her voice. She was very close to tears.

"It's not my fault, Gill. I don't want the Market torn down any more than you do!"

"Well, you must want it a little more than I do," Gillian countered, "because you managed to design the building Felix Cockrill plans to build to replace it with!"

"That's my job, Gill," said Jay sadly. "My job isn't doing what I want to do, it's doing what Felix tells me to do. You know that as well as anyone."

"There are other jobs. You could find one." She held up a hand that was shaking a little, as if to stave off his objection. "I don't want to go over all this again, Jay. I've got to go home." She turned and walked towards the stairway leading down to the ground level. Jackie followed, then turned back to see Jay Garnett leaning wearily against the pillar, his broad shoulders slumped in sorrow.

"Now there's an unhappy young man," Frances commented when they had descended the stairs and were walking toward one of the big exit doors that had originally been intended to admit horse-drawn farm wagons.

"Well, there's nothing I can do about that," said Gillian, but she sounded close to tears. "Jay made his decision, and I made mine." She didn't seem to be remotely happy about it though, Jackie noted.

No wonder Jay Garnett had said that Market Place was the worst thing that had ever happened to him. Evidently it had come between him and Gillian, and she refused to be swayed by his protestations of good intent. Jackie wished there were something she could do—she liked both these people, and it seemed obvious they were crazy about one another. Damn, but life was sad sometimes.

The phone by her bedside shrilled at her, had already rung, she now realized, several times. Groggily, she reached for it and fumbled it to somewhere in the neighborhood of her ear. "Uh. Yeah?"

"Jackie, it's Tom. Someone just tried to burn down the Kennel!"

CHAPTER 10

"Are you all right?"

"I'm fine. Everything's fine, but . . ."

"I'll be right there!" Jackie said, tossing the phone down and throwing aside the blankets. She turned on the bedside lamp and glanced at the clock. Just short of two A.M.

She was into her jeans, a shirt and some shoes and out the bedroom door in less than a minute, Jake at her heels, and Charlie at his. She paused and pushed open the door to Peter's room. He was sprawled out on his bed, dead to the world. Jackie decided not to wake him.

Jake seemed to sense something exciting in the air, and trotted off to retrieve his heavy leather lead from a hook near the kitchen door that led to the apartment's back yard. He came back into the front room, Charlie bouncing along behind him, as she wrote a note for Peter and unbolted the front door. Jake dropped the lead at his feet and sat patiently by the door. Charlie rubbed up against his front legs and purred.

"Of course you can come with me, Jake," she assured him, clipping on the lead. "Unfortunately, Charlie, you can't."

She grabbed a fluorescent-colored ping-pong ball from the floor and tossed it across the room. Charlie bounded after it, predictably, as it bounced across the hardwood floor. Jackie made good her escape, letting herself and Jake

out the door, and locking it behind them. She opened the
rear door of the car and Jake jumped inside and sat down
on the back seat.

Jackie unlocked the driver's side door and belted herself
in. Her hands trembled as she tried to find the ignition with
the tip of the key. She hadn't allowed herself to think since
hanging up the phone, but now all sorts of things were
running through her head. Tom was all right, but what if
he hadn't been? What if something had happened to him?
What if . . .

She didn't let herself get any further with that thought.
The key went into the ignition and she started the car, put
it in gear, and backed out of her tiny one-car garage as
carefully as she could with arms and legs that wouldn't
seem to stop shaking.

The bitter smell of burning wood and paint filled the air
around the kennel as Jackie pulled up into the long, curving
drive and maneuvered her way around two parked fire
trucks to find an empty spot large enough to park the Blazer
in.

From what she could see, the damage was slight and
confined to the outside of the building. Fire hoses were still
snaked out over the lawn, but the fire had been extinguished
and the water turned off. Firemen walked here and there in
the glow of the flashing lights from the fire trucks and
bright electric lanterns, finding hot spots and spraying them
with hand-held extinguishers. Dogs barked, howled, bayed,
and whined from the inside of the damaged kennel building.

Tom came rushing up to meet her as she stepped down
from the car. "I'm so glad you're here," he told her, holding her tight. "Grania's over there by the big tree. She's
fine, but a little shook up."

Jackie opened the back door and took the end of Jake's
lead. He hopped out of the car and walked obediently behind her, though he was quivering with what looked like
eagerness to investigate the scene the best way he knew
how—with his nose. "Come on, boy," Jackie told him,

giving his big head a pat. "Let's go see Grania."

Grania Cusack was a very self-assured young woman of thirteen, but as she stood under the big, spreading oak tree between her house and the smoking kennel building in her robe and slippers, she looked like a scared little girl. As soon as she saw Jackie she came up and put her arms around her, then reached down and petted Jake's head. Jake panted a friendly hello, then turned his attention back to the scene of the excitement.

"Why would anyone want to hurt us or the dogs, Jackie?" Grania asked. She looked up at Jackie, her green eyes troubled and slightly tearful.

"Maybe no one did, honey. Maybe it was an accident," Jackie suggested, but when she looked over at Tom he was shaking his head.

"I wish I thought that were true," he said, "but I'm pretty sure someone set the fire deliberately."

A siren added to the general chaos of the scene, and Bernie Youngquist's little white car, with a spinning red light perched on its roof, pulled into the driveway behind the fire trucks. Bernie climbed out of the car and came hurrying up to them.

"Tom," said Bernie, slightly out of breath. "I got here as quickly as I could. Is everyone all right? Hi, Jackie."

Jackie nodded a greeting, but was unprepared for how deeply unhappy she was to see Bernie Youngquist here right now. There was no good reason for it, but she could feel jealousy welling up inside her, and she didn't much like it. She didn't much like the image of Bernie coming to Tom's rescue. That was Jackie's job.

"We're all fine," Tom told Bernie. "The fire didn't come close to the house, and didn't do that much damage to the kennel. The dogs got a little shook up, but Joseph's been in there talking to them, and we've got fans going, clearing their air."

"And our little friend, Arlo?"

"Oh, he's taking all the confusion in stride compared to the rest," said Tom with a smile. "I think life on the streets has made a pretty tough dog out of that little character."

"Hi, Jackie," Bernie said. "We meet again."

"I guess we just travel in the same circles," Jackie commented. Jackie realized that Bernie must have been in touch with Tom since she was here this afternoon, for her to have learned the dog's name. That thought didn't do much to improve her already questionable mood.

"Evan sent me to get a look at the scene in case it turns out to be arson," Bernie said to Tom. "Is that what you think?"

"Well, it's what the firefighters think that's going to count," said Tom, "but Joseph and I had to quiet the dogs down a couple of times tonight before this happened. We thought it was probably raccoons or possums on the grounds, but we didn't find any when we came out to look around. Usually they go looking for garbage near the house, and leave the kennels alone, anyhow. The smell of the dogs scares them off. I think it might have been someone snooping around the place."

"But you didn't actually see anyone?"

"No. As you can see, there are a lot of trees and little outbuildings for someone to hide behind." He indicated the grounds of the kennels with a wave of his hand. "So I guess it's possible for someone to have been out here and neither of us to have seen them."

The two of them had turned away from Jackie and Grania and begun to walk in the direction of the kennel. Jackie followed, her arm still around Grania's shoulder, feeling more than a little left out of things. Jake moved into step behind her.

Bernie reached into her jacket pocket and withdrew a small spiral notebook and a silver pen. "Do you know anyone who'd want to harm you or your kennels? Enemies? Business rivals, perhaps?"

"I don't think I've been in town long enough to make any enemies," said Tom.

"Oh, you'd be surprised how short a time that can take," said Bernie with a smile. "I can name five or six people in the Palmer Police Department who wouldn't mind seeing *my* house burned down."

Bernie continued to ask questions and take down Tom's answers as they walked slowly across the grounds toward the kennel building, with Jackie and Grania and Jake bringing up the rear. Once Bernie stumbled slightly against a little hillock on the ground, and Tom put out an arm to steady her. Jackie felt an awful pang in her gut. She had to take a couple of deep breaths and get hold of herself.

Jake nuzzled her hand and whined softly. He seemed to sense her distress, though Jackie doubted her four-legged pal understood the complexity of her emotions right now. Lucky dog.

But then, Jackie couldn't really claim to understand them herself, she realized. Was she afraid that Tom was attracted to Bernie? Well, what man wouldn't be? Bernie Youngquist was about as close to perfection as Jackie could imagine a woman being, like a pretty porcelain doll. Jackie couldn't begin to look like that no matter how hard she tried, and she'd certainly never let it bother her before.

Was she worried that she was inadequate in some way, and that Tom would naturally be thinking about other women? Was she afraid she might be driving him into someone else's arms with her indecision about where their relationship should go from here? All of that, she supposed, and probably a few other things thrown in besides.

As they approached the damaged building, Jake strained at his lead, ears held up and nose high. "Looks like he might have some ideas about this situation," said Bernie, pointing at Jake. "It's just too bad he can't talk, huh?"

"Fortunately for us, Jake doesn't have to talk to do what he does best," said Tom. "Can I borrow him for a minute?" he asked Jackie.

"Sure." Jackie handed him the lead.

"Come on, Jake," said Tom, urging the big shepherd forward. "Let's go to work."

The man and the dog walked purposefully toward the kennel building, skirting firefighters carefully winding up lengths of heavy canvas hose as Jake described a zigzag pattern Jackie had seen before, trying to pick a scent out of the confusion of smoke and the smell of all the feet that had trampled through here since the fire department had arrived. Tom let him go to the end of the lead, but stayed right behind him, sometimes running to keep up.

Suddenly Jake stopped, quivering, and took off at right angles to his previous path, dragging Tom along. He sniffed the air eagerly, but instead of narrowing in on the source of the scent as Jackie had seen him do before, he went wider and wider, searching for the elusive trail of clues only he could read.

"Well, it looks like Jake is on the job," Bernie commented as she watched them walk back and forth across the kennel grounds. "They seem to work pretty well together."

"Oh, they're old hands at this sort of thing," Jackie told her.

"Jake saved my life last spring," Grania informed Bernie.

Bernie's eyebrows shot up in surprise. On her, even such a comical gesture seemed strangely graceful. "I guess this is a story Evan didn't tell me."

The implication was, of course, that Evan Stillman had told the new detective plenty of other stories about Jackie. He probably hadn't mentioned the events of the previous spring because he hadn't had any part in solving the crimes involved. That sort of thing tended to make Evan just a little testy.

"It's a little complicated. I'll tell you all about it sometime," Jackie said. "The important thing is we all escaped unharmed—with Jake's help, of course." She smiled down at Grania.

Grania grinned back. The trauma of the experience far behind her, Tom's teenage daughter rather seemed to enjoy remembering the adventurous aspects of that eventful Saturday night last spring. It was less like real life in some ways than it was like a movie, even to Jackie.

"That's some dog you've got there," said Bernie. "And some guy."

"Well, if there's a relevant scent out there, Jake and Tom will find it," Jackie told Bernie. "When Jake gets through he'll know more than you or I or the firefighters about what happened here tonight. The problem is, I guess, that because he's a dog, he doesn't have any way to tell us what it all means."

"I guess I'd better go talk to the firefighters before they leave," said Bernie. "I'm sure they have some valuable opinions about the cause of this fire that'll be a help to me. Tell Tom I'll have more questions for him later."

"Sure thing," said Jackie. "I think Grania and I'll go inside and have a cup of hot chocolate. You can join us when you get through here, if you like." She had felt like she ought to add that last, but she was trying to be sincere. Bernie Youngquist was a perfectly nice person—it wasn't her fault she was perfect.

"Thanks. Maybe I will." She gave Jackie a grateful smile. Jackie was taken aback by the sudden realization that people who were perceived as so far above them by others probably didn't have all that many friends. Maybe Bernie's kind of beauty had its drawbacks as well as its obvious advantages.

"Jackie. Wake up, babe."

"Huh?" Jackie looked up to see Tom standing over her, his hair wet from the shower. Jake was lying down on the rug in the middle of the floor, and Grania was asleep on the other end of the long sofa in Tom's living room. "You smell like smoke."

"You should have smelled me *before* the shower," said Tom. "Well, come to think of it, maybe not," he amended with a wry smile.

"I guess I fell asleep," Jackie said, sitting up and stretching. "I should probably be going. What time is it, anyhow?"

"About four, I think. Let me get my darling daughter to bed. I'll be right back."

He scooped Grania up in his arms and carried her into her room. He was back a minute later. He sat down next to Jackie and drew her close. "What time does Peter get up?" he asked.

"On a Saturday? Not until he absolutely has to. Of course he has to be at the dojo at ten."

Tom nodded. "Grania, too. That still gives us five hours."

"Not what I'd call a lot of sleep," said Jackie, nuzzling into the crook of his arm.

"Who said anything about sleep?"

CHAPTER 11

Jackie and Tom watched their teenage children, dressed in white *gi* and soft-soled Chinese slippers, and carrying identical black gym bags, disappear inside the Sixteenth Street Kenpo Dojo, where they'd be happy as clams doing *kata* and kicking butt for the next three hours. "I don't know about you," said Tom, "but I'm starving to death. Did you say Frances was waiting for us at Miranda's?"

"Waiting for us, yes. Waiting to eat, probably not. Shall we go while there might still be some food left?"

Tom and Jackie were united in their dislike of the sort of endlessly cloned coffee shops that sprang up like opportunistic fungus at the bottoms of interstate offramps. They frequently went out to breakfast on Saturdays, and had accumulated a small but respectable collection of favorite breakfast places, including a seedy-looking roadhouse not far down the highway from Cusack Kennels, and Miranda's Healthy Stuff Café in downtown Palmer's Market District.

Miranda's was known throughout Palmer as the home of the most delicious breakfasts in town. Menu items like Miranda's Mushroom, Spinach, and Brie Omelet, accompanied by inch-thick slices of homemade whole-wheat bread and bottomless glasses of fresh-squeezed orange juice, brought weekend breakfasters into town from suburbs far and near to compete for seating with disgruntled downtown residents who heartily wished the word hadn't gotten out.

Jackie and Tom didn't need to be disgruntled this morning, as Frances had arrived early and secured a table for them, and they walked past the crowd of hungry people waiting just outside the door, as well as the crowd of hungrier people waiting just inside the door, and sat down in a little upholstered booth adorned with hammered silver tacks and overhung with an industrial-looking conical light fixture.

"And I hope you two appreciate it, too!" said Frances when they sat down. "I even waited to order, except for this insignificant little appetizer of fresh fruit compote."

"Which you're willing to share, right?" Jackie raised one eyebrow in a gesture that never seemed to intimidate Frances Costello, probably because Jackie had learned it from her over the course of her childhood. It used to send chills up Jackie's spine when she was a kid, and it seemed to work pretty well on Peter, too.

"Of course I am, dearest daughter. Grab a couple of forks and dig in, kids. The waitress'll have to notice us sooner or later."

Jackie sat down and leaned into the corner of the booth, stifling a yawn with the back of her hand. Tom put his head back and closed his eyes.

"Well," said Frances, "you two seem to be a little short on sleep this morning."

"Well, the fire kept us up late," Jackie informed her. She had already given her mother the short version of the kennel fire this morning on the phone. Of course the fire wasn't the only thing that had cost her sleep last night, but some things were none of her mother's business.

"I'm just glad no one was hurt," said Frances, "and that there wasn't much damage."

"Me too. So what kind of trouble have you been getting into since I saw you last, Frances my dear?" Tom asked with a smile.

"Ancestor trouble," said Frances, eyeing Jackie. "I've uncovered a sort of a black sheep in the Costello line."

"Well, what's an Irish family without a few of those?"

Tom asked her. "There are a few Cusacks and Maddens with checkered pasts, I can assure you. In fact, my mother's mother's cousin was a famous gangster in Hell's Kitchen."

"You're related to Owney Madden?" Frances asked in a voice tinged with a lot of surprise and not a little admiration.

"That's the one," said Tom. "Bob Hoskins played him in *The Cotton Club*," he told Jackie.

"Oh, don't try to impress Jackie with a gangster for a cousin," Frances advised him, "even one with film credits. She's not exactly thrilled with this whole black sheep business. I don't think she believes it enriches the roots of her family tree."

"It was just sort of a shock to find out that my father's grandfather had a price on his head, that's all," Jackie explained. "And your gangster cousin probably got whacked by some rival gang leader in an alley. What's so enriching about that?"

"Actually, he sold all his crime-related interests, retired to upstate New York with his wife and children, and lived to a ripe old age," Tom informed her.

Jackie had to laugh. "Okay, score one for you and Owney Madden. I'll even admit it's sort of interesting having colorful characters in my ancestry," she admitted, "but I worry about Peter glamorizing people like Great-grandfather Costello because of what they did wrong rather than what they might have done right."

"It's a matter of viewpoint, Jacqueline," her mother informed her calmly. "Fighting the English was never considered a crime in Ireland."

"Except by the English," Jackie reminded her with a perfectly straight face.

"Well, yes, I suppose them," Frances allowed with a dismissive flip of the hand. "But in the end the Irish did secure their independence and their island, or most of it, anyway. And it was people like Michael Costello who helped set the stage for that, even though those earlier revolts were less than successful. He left Ireland in a hurry," Frances said, punctuating her point with a wagging finger, "but you may be sure he didn't leave in disgrace. His family was very proud of him."

Their server, a harried woman named Doris who had been at this for four hours already, finally made it to their table, and they ordered omelets and wheat toast all around. "And water for everyone," Frances told her. "Price is absolutely no object when I'm buying breakfast for my family."

"That's why she wants us all to have some of your wonderful orange juice, too," Jackie informed Doris. Doris made a note of it, winked at Jackie, and went to put in their order. Frances raised an eyebrow. Her daughter ignored it, and felt a real sense of satisfaction. She must be growing up.

"At least we've all got family to look after us," said Frances. "Not like that poor woman who died in the alley the other night."

"Her name was Rosie Canty," Jackie said. "Is that an Irish name, Mother?"

"Lots of Cantys in Cork, I seem to remember," said Frances, who devoured books on Irish families the way some women devoured paperback romances. "And it seems familiar to me, too. Maybe I knew someone by that name once—I can't seem to remember them, though, if I did." She frowned with the mental effort, then sighed. "But I guess I should expect a few lapses in memory at my age," she allowed.

"Oh, Mother, you're not old," Jackie told her. "And don't the Cooleys live practically forever?"

"Practically," Frances agreed. "And they make trouble 'til the very last, too. We're that kind of family. Ah, well, it'll come to me eventually," she said. "It always does."

"Don't you often wonder, when you see people living on the street," Jackie mused, "where *their* families could be?"

"Yes," said Tom. "I sometimes think about whether someone's wondering where they are right now, or if there's no one to care about them at all. Don't they have families, or are they the skeletons and black sheep in their families' closets?''

Jackie sighed. ''I wonder if people like the Cockrills who've probably been here since before the Revolution have skeletons and black sheep in their closets, or if it's just immigrants like us who are so all-fired interesting.''

''The Cockrills are just as much immigrants on this soil as you or your great-grandparents, dear daughter—they just got off a slightly earlier boat. And you may be sure they have their share of secrets, too,'' her mother said. ''In fact, I wouldn't be at all surprised if that mousy little Emma weren't a black sheep in her own fashion.''

''Oh, come on, Mother! Emma Cockrill? You can't be serious! I'd be willing to bet you ten dollars that she's never done anything remotely rebellious in her entire life!''

''Don't be too sure,'' said Frances. ''And let's make that twenty dollars. Stop and consider the matter of her younger sister, Eden.''

''Okay, I considered it. So what?''

''Consider the difference in their ages.''

''Twenty years, give or take.''

''And how old would you say Ada Cockrill is?''

Jackie dredged up memories of Ada Cockrill's picture in the *Gazette*, and her occasional appearance on local television on behalf of some charity or other. ''Well-preserved, but probably around seventy.''

''Don't you think that's a tad too old to have a twenty-year-old daughter?''

''It seems to be, but maybe it runs in the family. You've seen her brother—the man who was talking to Gillian after the meeting? He can't be more than about thirty-six.''

''Well, it may not mean anything at all, but in my day it was not unknown for a mother to adopt her young daughter's—shall we say, inconvenient—offspring, after going off for a long stay out of town with the daughter in question, and pass her grandchild off as her own baby.''

''I never heard of such a thing,'' Jackie told her mother.

''It was probably a lot more common than anyone let on, and likely more common, then *or* now, than having a child of your own at fifty," said Frances. "And there's Emma still at home with Mom and Dad, just possibly serving out some penance she's placed on herself for having a child out of wedlock."

"Mother, it's the twentieth century. Get real, for heaven's sake!"

"Well, it may not be as late in the century for the Cockrills as it is for you and I, darling daughter," Frances informed Jackie. "They're an old-fashioned family, and Emma is an old-fashioned woman, and frankly, I don't consider the idea all that far-fetched."

"You know, I think Frances may have a point," Tom said.

"I'll grudgingly admit that," said Jackie, crossing her arms in front of her chest. It was a gesture she often found herself using around her mother when she knew she was losing an argument, which was pretty often, all things considered.

"Well, I've been right a time or two," Frances allowed, "but it's all just pointless gossip, I suppose. Let's talk about something more useful. What did the firefighters say about your fire?" she asked Tom.

"They think it was started when somebody poured fuel of some kind onto the side of the building," Tom told her. "The police couldn't find any footprints, or rather they could find thousands of them, but who could tell which ones might have been left by the person who started the fire? They'll have more details for me after an inspector's gone over the scene."

"Did Jake find anything interesting?" Jackie asked, remembering the two of them tramping over the grounds the night before.

"He got awfully excited at one particular scent out on the perimeter of the property," Tom recalled. "But it seemed to peter out before he could get a lock on it. We went back and forth over the area, but it was all too confusing with all those people milling around, and the smell of the fire, and all the other dogs." He smiled at Jackie. "Jake's a terrific tracker, but even he has his limits."

"I'm just surprised Marcella Jacobs didn't show up in the middle of all the rest of it," said Jackie. "She's been turning up everywhere else I've gone the past couple of days." She craned her neck, looking all around to make sure the reporter in question wasn't even now getting ready to pop up and shout "Surprise!"

"Well, there was no dead body involved, and Tom's business is situated too far from downtown Palmer to have been associated in any way with the Market Place issue," said Frances thoughtfully, "so I suppose she couldn't be bothered with it."

"I suppose you're right."

"That's twice in two minutes," said Frances with satisfaction.

"But I'll bet her coverage of the Save the Market meeting really stirred up something in the Cockrill household," said Jackie. "I wouldn't want to be within a mile of Felix and Ada Cockrill tomorrow when they catch sight of Marcella's article and the picture of Emma and Eden at the Save the Market meeting."

"Me neither," Frances agreed. "Especially if Felix is as frightening as Gillian Zane seems to think he is."

Jackie and Tom arrived at her place a little later to pick up Jake for an afternoon romp in the park with Peter and Grania. Jackie went to let Jake in through the kitchen doorway from the back yard.

"Your message light's blinking," Tom told her when she and Jake came back in from the kitchen.

Jackie reached for Jake's lead, hanging near the door. "Just punch that big button," she told him, "I can hear the speaker from in here."

"Jackie, it's Emma Cockrill," said the voice on the other end of the phone. "I . . . I don't know if you're free tomorrow, that is whether or not you have something else you'd rather do, but I certainly hope you are. Free, that is. I wonder if . . . if you'd like to join my family and me for Sunday brunch?"

CHAPTER 12

Jackie surveyed her closet with a frown. Sunday morning had sneaked right up on her without an answer to the burning question: what does one wear to a Sunday brunch with one of the oldest, richest, and most powerful families in Palmer, Ohio?

Jackie's usual Sunday brunch uniform was blue jeans, a T-shirt, and a vest or blazer, but that would never do. She reached for her black rayon dress, usually handy on a peg by the closet door, but when her hand closed on empty air, she realized she hadn't picked it up from the cleaners on Friday. Perfect. Now what?

Jackie had to admit to herself, as she peered into her bedroom closet with diminishing hope, that she was probably being used. She wasn't Emma Cockrill's friend—indeed, she'd be surprised to learn that someone as introverted and socially awkward as Emma actually *had* a friend—and in truth she was scarcely even an acquaintance.

Jackie traveled so far outside the Cockrills' social circles, in fact, that she might as well be living on another planet rather than in the same middle-sized city as far as the likelihood of accidentally running into them.

As far as money was concerned, the largest amount she ever saw was the positive balance in her checkbook for the few hours between depositing her check from the University and paying her bills. Felix and Ada Cockrill's life of exclusive clubs and trendy charities was as foreign to her as Stone Age tribes in New Guinea. No, *more* foreign. At least Stone Age New Guineans had to struggle to make ends meet just like she did.

The very farthest reaches of the closet bar, back where the glow from the single lightbulb never quite reached, were packed tight with hangers holding the clothes she never seemed to wear, and it looked like it was time to brave the unexplored territories and find out once and for all what was actually in there. "Come on, Jackie—show some courage here," she exhorted herself. She took a deep breath and reached for a handful of hangers.

Jeez, she thought to herself as she peered through plastic dry-cleaning bags. Some of this stuff dated back to her stint in the suburbs with Cooper Walsh. What had possessed her to hang on to so much stuff she didn't need? She had gotten rid of her philandering husband more than three years ago— it was time most of these clothes went the same route.

Two hours later Jackie had separated the contents of her closet into stuff that she might actually wear someday, stuff she really must give away someday soon, and stuff she'd forgotten she owned but decided she liked. What she hadn't done was decide on an outfit for brunch at the Cockrills'. She stood in the midst of three piles of clothing and took a deep breath.

"Peter!"

"Yeah, Mom!"

"What are you doing?"

"I was just downloading some genealogy files from the Web."

"Come in here and help me before you discover an ax murderer among our distinguished ancestors, please."

Peter came into the room a moment later. Jake walked in behind him and lay down on a pile of clothing. "Cripes, Mom, and you're always on me about my room! Look at this place! Don't you ever hang anything up?"

"Very funny. Now here's my problem. I'm going to brunch at the Cockrills' in an hour."

"Who the heck are the Cockrills?" Peter wanted to know.

"You know—Cockrill Industries, Cockrill Financial Services, Cockrill Park?"

"Yeah, I guess so." He thought about it briefly. "They're rich, right?"

"Filthy."

"So that's their problem. What's yours?"

"I can't make up my mind what to wear."

"You mean I get to decide?"

"I'm desperate. Sue me."

"Okay, I choose thrashed jeans and an Ozzy Osbourne T-shirt. That way nobody else there will be wearing the same outfit you are, and you won't get all embarrassed and stuff."

Jackie pointed to two dresses on the bed. "Choose between those, Mister Wiseguy."

"I was going to loan you the shirt," said Peter, obviously disappointed. "It's even clean. I think. Nearly."

"Ahem."

Peter looked over the two dresses. "The green one, then."

"You're sure? You don't think maybe the pink one would be better?"

"Pink bites. Green is your favorite color." He gave her a warning look as she wavered. "You said I could choose."

"You're right," said Jackie. She threw the pink dress on the giveaway pile. "Pink definitely bites. Thanks, Peter." Now all she had to do was decide on the shoes.

Felix and Ada Cockrill's palatial three-story home was situated on a series of gently rolling little hills on the northernmost edge of Palmer, in a neighborhood of rambling estates the size of small counties. A veritable forest of hardwoods surrounded it on all sides, ceasing abruptly a hundred yards from the house itself to make way for a huge and painfully perfect green lawn interspersed with various gardens.

Jackie parked her Blazer in the immaculate white gravel

of the wide drive encircling a fountain that would have been right at home in the center of Rome, and walked up seven marble steps to the door.

From a distance, somewhere inside the house, Jackie could hear the sound of a man shouting at the top of his lungs. The words, mercifully, were unintelligible, but the voice was very deep and commanding, even without words. The frightening Mr. Felix Cockrill, perhaps? Fighting an impulse to run back down the stairs and drive back to her apartment as fast as she could, she looked for the doorbell.

A deep bonging accompanied her tentative pressure on the white button set into a gold filigree on the door frame, and the voice stopped abruptly. Jackie could hear footsteps tapping toward her, and a moment later the door was pulled open by a tall maid in a dove-gray uniform.

Jackie was lamenting her lack of formal calling cards and opening her mouth to introduce herself when Emma Cockrill, exceedingly proper in a dark sprigged dress with a white collar, and a delicate jeweled brooch, ducked under the maid's arm and through the door, and whisked Jackie away and down the steps. Her hand on Jackie's arm trembled just a bit.

"Would you like to walk around the grounds for a few minutes?" Emma asked her. "They'll call us when it's time to eat, won't you, Mona?"

"We will, Miss Emma."

"Shall we, then? I think it's the loveliest day for a walk, don't you?" She turned anxious eyes on Jackie as if fearing she'd refuse the offer and insist on being seen into the house.

"Sure," Jackie replied. "I'd love to." She'd love to be as far as possible from whoever it was inside that house who was angry enough to shout that loud, that was for sure. And it was a beautiful day, no doubt about it. The bitter cold of only a few days before had gradually settled back into a pleasant coolness yesterday, and by this morning Ohio was in the gentle grip of a full-fledged Indian summer.

A formal rose garden occupied the area in front of the house, with paths laid out straight as rulers between care-

fully trimmed bushes and globular trees and arbors and trel-
lises crowded with climbing roses. "This is Mother's
garden," said Emma. "Of course she has a man to take
care of it."

"Of course," said Jackie, and hoped that hadn't come
out as sarcastic as it had felt. "It's very beautiful. I've
always loved roses."

"She's forever fiddling with the design," Emma went
on, "having one variety removed and another planted, or
taking out all the benches, or ordering all new statuary. It's
a passion with her."

She led Jackie down a path of tightly placed cement flag-
stones in the shape of full-blown blooms and through an
arbor trailing deep red flowers, a surprising number for the
time of year. Jackie congratulated Ada Cockrill's gardener
for his abilities, though the garden's design seemed overly
stiff and artificial.

They walked through a double row of gigantic rose
bushes like something out of one of the darker chapters of
Alice in Wonderland, and out a white garden gate to the
lawn beyond. "The entire Cockrill family gardens, you
know," Emma told Jackie, "even Father. The Japanese
garden on the east side of the house is his, and that one
over there is mine."

Orderly rows of dwarf fruit trees and berry hedges occupied the area Emma was indicating on the west side of
the house. It was smaller than the rose garden, almost
cramped, even though it was surrounded by nothing more
than more acres of useless lawn. It was almost as though
Emma felt she ought not to take up too much space with
anything as inconsequential as her own garden.

Jackie walked toward Emma's garden, and Emma followed. "That reporter said you were a detective," Emma
ventured. "Do you work for the police department? I
thought Eden said you were an instructor at the University." She sounded confused, Jackie thought. Well, join the
club, Emma.

"I'm not really a detective," she told her. "I used to
date a detective on the Palmer force, a man by the name

of Michael McGowan, and I guess you could say I've managed to get myself into the thick of a few criminal cases around town the past few years, but it's not exactly the same thing.''

She eyed a raspberry hedge, the berries long gone now, but still prickly with tiny thorns. ''Ah, that must be the one that bit you,'' she remarked.

Emma's hand flew to her bandaged arm. ''The raspberry cane! Oh, my, yes! They can be ferocious.'' She tittered nervously. It was obvious Emma wasn't practiced at entertaining guests, and whatever situation it was that still lurked back there in the big house wasn't helping out much.

Jackie felt sorry for Emma, which was the whole reason she'd accepted the invitation, she realized. Maybe not the greatest reason to spend several precious weekend hours being bored or worse in the Cockrill mansion, but it made her feel like a better person, and with the unworthy feelings she'd been having lately about Bernie Youngquist, she needed all the help she could possibly get in that department.

They walked around the back of the house to the east, and were greeted by Felix Cockrill's elegant Japanese garden, laid out with mossy boulders and meandering paths surrounding a huge pond with willows and weeping blue cedars bending down to the water's edge. Koi of every possible color and combination swam up to them in anticipation of a feeding, touching the surface of the water with their delicate mouths.

Emma opened up a dark green cabinet carefully hidden in one of the bushes near the edge of the pond and took out a container of fish food. She tossed handfuls of it to the Koi, who churned the water as they swam this way and that, gulping it down. ''They eat out of Father's hand,'' she told Jackie, ''but I've never learned to make them trust me in quite the same way.''

''Does your father have a man to do his garden, too?'' Jackie asked Emma.

Emma put the fish food back into the cabinet and walked away from the pond, with Jackie following. ''He used to do it all himself,'' she said sadly, ''but his hands have become very crippled.'' She held out her own thin, pale hands and turned them slowly around in the sunlight as if envisioning them like her father's. After a few moments she put them behind her back and continued walking.

''I suppose your father has seen the article in today's Palmer *Gazette*,'' Jackie said, as gently as she could manage. She didn't want to be rude, but she also didn't want to walk into that house without knowing what to expect.

Emma nodded. ''He's terribly unhappy about it. Mother too. How I wish I'd never let Eden talk me into going to that meeting! I told her it was a terrible idea, but she wouldn't hear of not going.''

''Well, at least you can share the blame,'' said Jackie. ''I used to wish I had a brother or sister sometimes when my mother was mad at me. Being an only child also meant being the only one available to take the heat.''

''Oh, Father's never really angry with Eden,'' said Emma. ''He tries, but he can't really manage it. Even when he found out it was her idea to go to the meeting, he wasn't really angry with her.''

''But he was with you?'' Jackie asked, picking up on something in Emma's tone of voice.

Emma looked up at her, a bitter half-smile forming on her thin lips. ''Father's never found it difficult to be angry with me,'' she said.

She turned and walked away from the Japanese garden. Jackie followed.

''Does your sister have a garden, too?''

''My sister?''

''Eden, I mean.''

''Oh, yes, Eden has a garden.'' Emma smiled, seeming to forget her earlier distress. ''It's the loveliest place—the bane of Mother's existence. Come along—I'll show you.''

They walked around to the rear of the house, then away from it on a graveled path that led almost to the line of dark trees surrounding the manicured grounds. A small, cheery cottage painted a pale yellow with white trim peeked out from the shadows of the trees. Around it grew a riotous garden of dozens, maybe hundreds, of annuals and perennials in every conceivable color, seemingly sowed at random and left to grow where they fell. The effect was a merry one, Jackie thought, and was in fact less chaotic than it seemed at first glance.

"Eden's cottage garden," said Emma. "She wanted to put it on the fourth side of the house, but Mother put her foot down and told Eden she'd have to put it out here. So Eden fixed up the cottage and moved herself out here, too. Isn't that so like her?" Admiration fought it out with envy in Emma's voice. "Eden's so brave."

"Don't you think you're brave, too?" Jackie asked Emma. "I mean, you went to that Save the Market meeting even though you knew your parents wouldn't approve."

Jackie felt like an idiot discussing parental approval with a forty-year-old woman, but in Emma's case it really didn't seem irrelevant. In many ways she was more like a little girl than a grown woman.

"Oh, you see, that was Eden being courageous as usual, and me being dragged along. Eden's always trying to get me out of my shell, you know." She studied her sturdy shoes for at least half a minute as if there might be something important written on them, then she sighed loudly. "But it's such a comfortable shell sometimes, you know? And look at all the trouble Eden's caused this time!"

From the main house a bell sounded, as if over a loudspeaker hidden somewhere on the grounds. "That's for us," said Emma, glancing nervously at the house in the distance. "I suppose we mustn't keep Mother and Father waiting." She walked briskly back towards the big house. Jackie managed to keep up with her, and was grateful she'd chosen the comfortable shoes.

CHAPTER 13

"Emma tells us you work for Rodgers University," said Ada Cockrill. Ada was showing Jackie to her place at a long table in the Cockrills' formal dining room, which wasn't a lot smaller than the ground floor of Jackie's apartment, and a lot more expensively furnished. Emma trailed along behind her mother, small and silent. "You're an instructor there, is that correct?"

"That's right," Jackie replied. She sat down at a place on one side of the table, and Ada walked around to the other side, still trailing Emma like a train. Jackie's place, like all the places at the table, was laid with gleaming silver and delicate floral bone china, decorated with a tiny willow basket of fresh fall flowers, and marked with a hand-written place card showing her name in elaborate lavender script. "I teach film," Jackie said finally, when she remembered there had been a question asked.

"You must have a very creative nature," Ada remarked as she took her own seat. Jackie could almost swear she heard an echo, the ceiling in here was so high. She checked surreptitiously for colonies of bats in the rafters. There were none in evidence, but they might have been sleeping, for all she knew.

"Well, I seem to spend more energy telling students about other people's creative ventures than launching my own," Jackie replied, looking around at the walls and fur-

86

nishings as casually as she could manage, "but I used to write for television, once upon a time."

"Oh," said Ada, picking up her napkin and shaking out the elaborate folds some servant had gone to the trouble to put into it. "How interesting." She smiled a little smile Jackie didn't believe before her face settled down into the same mask of not-quite-pleasant neutrality it had worn since she greeted Jackie and Emma at the door after their walk around the grounds.

Jackie was pretty sure Ada Cockrill didn't find her or her former writing career the least bit interesting, but Palmer's leading socialite and do-gooder was too steeped in etiquette to say so, and Jackie was thankful for that. Good manners were, as usual, greasing the ofttimes sticky wheels of human interaction.

There was an air in the Cockrill house of anger and unresolved issues that was thick enough to smell. Ada was suffering from it in her way, and Emma, who had taken a place next to her and now sat there hunched in fearful silence, in hers. Jackie picked up her own napkin, a huge square of heavy, ivory-colored damask, and unfolded it into her lap. It gave her something with which to fill a few awkward seconds.

Jackie had read Marcella's article in the *Sunday Palmer Gazette* that had landed on her porch at eight o'clock that morning, and seen the picture of the slightly startled Cockrill sisters that Marcella had been so proud of obtaining on Friday evening. She imagined that the angry voices she had heard coming from inside the Cockrill mansion earlier had had a lot to do with that particular photograph.

Marcella's piece had contained a great deal of arch humor at the expense of the Save the Market folks, making them sound a bit shrill and not a little pitiful for their desire to preserve their little portion of downtown Palmer from the sort of beneficial changes that Market Place would bring, in Marcella's opinion.

In Marcella's opinion (Jackie noted with amusement that it was never possible to say "Marcella's *humble* opinion") Market Place would allow a crumbling downtown neighborhood to be reborn and breathe new life and new dollars into the city. In Marcella's opinion Market Place was the greatest thing to hit the idea of city planning since the invention of running water.

There had been some pithy quotes, too, from Mayor Jane Bellamy, about the new era Palmer was entering—the revitalization of the Market District that Market Place would bring, and the leaving behind of urban blight, and not a little about the outdated notions to which some people persisted in clinging to about preservation for its own sake.

"Just because something's old," said Mayor Bellamy, "doesn't mean it ought to be hung onto past its usefulness." Jackie had wondered if she'd still be saying that when *she* was old. In Jackie's opinion the Mayor was already useless.

Jackie peeked discreetly at the place cards on either side of her to determine who she'd be eating with today. It would be Eden Cockrill on her left, it appeared, and Jay Garnett on her right. She hoped they'd show up soon. She didn't feel like she had anything very interesting to say to Ada Cockrill, and Emma was tucked up into herself like a lace hanky in a lady's sleeve.

Ada Cockrill was well-preserved and extremely well taken care of, Jackie noted. She was a bit overdressed for any Sunday brunch in Jackie's experience, in a fawn-colored suit worn over a creamy silk lace blouse with elaborate ruffles at the neck and sleeves. An antique carnelian cameo brooch pinned down some of the ruffles, and matching earrings completed the look of upper-class perfection. Jackie was impressed with what the outfit must have cost, but she had to admit she wouldn't be caught dead in it herself.

She wasn't about to revise that estimate of Ada's age she had given Frances, either—not downward anyway, but it was evident that not only could the wealthy Mrs. Cockrill avail herself of the best skin and hair care money could buy, but she had also purchased some very classy cosmetic surgery somewhere along the way.

These things had a way of showing themselves if you

knew where to look. Ada's face was unnaturally tight under a deliberately casual coiffure of frosted blonde—in fact, it was at least a generation younger than either her neck or the backs of her hands. Her nails were long and lacquered to perfection in a dark burgundy shade. Her eyes were a deep, mossy green, and as hard as little stones.

Ada rang a silver bell that was sitting by her right hand, and the maid Jackie had seen earlier at the front door appeared at Ada's elbow. "See what's keeping the others, Mona," Ada requested.

"Yes, Ma'am," said Mona, and tap-tapped back over the huge expanse of polished hardwood floor and out the double doors.

"You have a lovely house," Jackie said, trying to get the conversation going again. "I've admired it many times from the highway."

"Thank you," Ada replied pleasantly. "It came to me from my parents. I've always been fond of it." She glanced toward the doorway, which remained stubbornly empty. She did not seem at all pleased by this, Jackie noted. Ada's parents, Jackie recalled, had been the ones with all the money. She wondered if that had been Felix's main motivation for marrying her.

"Your rose garden is very beautiful, too," she offered.

Ada looked back at her. "Oh, Emma showed you the rose garden." She smiled, a bit more genuinely than before. "I'm glad. I take a great deal of pride in it. I'm so happy you enjoyed it. I don't suppose you've had an opportunity to see the rest of the house?"

"No, I'm afraid not."

"I'm sure Emma will be happy to show you around before you go, won't you, Emma?"

Emma nodded, tortoise-like, from somewhere between her shoulder blades. Her mother's presence seemed to make her incapable of speech.

"Sorry we're late," said a bright voice from the doorway. Eden Cockrill came into the dining room with Jay Garnett, pulling him along by the sleeve of his tweed sport coat. "Uncle Jay was in a blue mood, and it fell to me to cheer him up a bit."

Jay Garnett didn't look terribly cheery from where Jackie was sitting, but he allowed himself to be pulled along to Jackie's side of the table with a measure of good humor. Jackie bet herself that the reason for his mood had red hair, owned a bookstore, and wasn't speaking to him. "We meet again," she said as he sat down next to her.

Jay seemed to notice her for the first time. "The lady from the Market! Jackie?"

"You remembered!"

"I always remember women who stomp all over my feet." His dark eyes twinkled, but the sadness never completely left them. "It's good to see you again, but I never thought I'd run into you in Ada's dining room."

"Ms. Walsh is Emma's guest today, Jay," Ada informed her brother. "They met at the Save the Market meeting on Friday night." Ada spoke the first part of her statement with good grace and good manners, but reserved an especially icy tone for the second part. Jackie could tell they were in for a rough ride at the dining table today.

"Well, Emma's got great taste in guests," Jay said, ignoring his sister's subtext and smiling. Emma smiled back at him, shyly, for just a split second before ducking her head again.

"Emma was quite impressed with Ms. Walsh the other night," said Eden from the other side of Jackie. "Weren't you, Em?"

Emma murmured something unintelligible without lifting up her face.

"The woman from the newspaper told us Ms. Walsh solves crimes," Eden continued, speaking to Jay and Ada. "Em's scarcely been able to stop talking about it ever since. You'll have to tell us some stories, Ms. Walsh," she insisted. "We'd love to hear all about it. It all sounds so exciting, doesn't it? Like television or the movies!"

"It doesn't amount to anything, really," said Jackie with a wave of her hand, but before Eden had time to object to her dismissal of the subject, a tall, white-haired man in a dark suit and tie strode into the room and took a seat at the opposite end of the table from Ada. Jackie realized as she tried to stop herself from staring at him open-mouthed that nothing amounted to anything much in the presence of Felix Cockrill, with the possible exception of Felix Cockrill himself.

Even sitting down, Felix Cockrill was tall and imposing, and at least as frightening as Gillian Zane had claimed. He was at least ten years older than his wife, though on him, eighty or so could scarcely be called old age. His limbs were long and spidery, his face was lined and craggy under a mane of thick, snowy hair, and his eyes were a piercing blue like the sting of an ice cube. They were the same color as Emma's eyes, Jackie noted, but the difference in the effect was the difference between predator and prey.

Felix Cockrill took a long look around at the table. The look he gave Emma burned with anger, and she seemed to shrink under it even more, if that were possible. As for his wife, he glanced over her as though he barely saw her and didn't much care whether or not he did. Jay Garnett got a grudging nod that seemed to convey respect, and Eden received a flash of genuine affection before her father frowned as though he had suddenly remembered he was unhappy with her. Finally his gaze came to rest on Jackie.

A heartbeat went by, then another, as Felix Cockrill's eyes seemed to burn into her. He seemed to grow taller and still more threatening, and Jackie could feel her eyes widening to take him all in as she burned in the blue fire of his eyes. Finally, he spoke in a low, rumbling voice. "I don't believe we've met. I'm Felix Cockrill."

Jackie swallowed. "I'm Jackie Walsh, Mr. Cockrill. I'm very pleased to meet you." Maybe not entirely honest, Jackie thought—but she could scarcely say she was very terrified to meet him, could she?

"The pleasure is all mine, Ms. Walsh." His wide mouth formed a smile full of big, white teeth, and his eyes crinkled pleasantly. "I'm always happy to meet my daughters' friends. Now, shall we eat?"

Jackie could feel herself slumping with relief that Felix

Cockrill hadn't actually eaten her alive on the spot. On the other hand, brunch wasn't over yet, she reminded herself.

A white-coated man entered the room carrying a bottle of champagne around the table, and pouring it into the long, pale green flutes that sat at each place. It smelled delightful, and Jackie decided to accept one glass, knowing she would be staying for a while after the meal.

"Aren't you having any?" she asked Emma, noticing her empty glass.

"No, I never do," said Emma, barely loud enough to be heard. "I can't."

Jackie felt terribly sorry for Emma, so overshadowed by the more powerful and more interesting members of her family. What chance did a quiet little woman like her have to shine in this group?

Felix brought his hands up to the table top to deal with his napkin, and Jackie noticed for the first time that they were crippled with arthritis, bent and knobby and nearly useless, seeming to belong to some other man entirely. It was the only obvious sign of disability connected to his age that she could detect.

Ada rang the little silver bell again, and two more white-coated servants materialized through a door in the wood paneling behind Felix with a wheeled cart, and began to serve dishes of hot and cold food. No one spoke as the dishes were laid out up and down the big table, but Jackie could see looks passing between Emma and Eden and their parents, and they were not happy looks by any stretch of the imagination.

All this tension should have robbed her of any appetite, but the wonderful smells emanating from the serving dishes was making her hungry, Jackie realized, and when the servants removed the covers it all looked more delicious than it smelled.

Jackie was known to invite friends and family over for Sunday brunch herself, but sometimes the menu consisted of You-Bake-It Pizza, and even when she cooked up the meal from scratch, she thought a bit sadly, somehow the results never looked quite like this.

"My wife tells me that you met my daughters at a meeting opposing the Market Place project," said Felix, as casually as if he were discussing the state of the weather in central Ohio.

Jackie decided she might as well answer just as casually. "Yes, that's right—the meeting at the bookstore in Farmers and Growers Friday night."

She glanced at Emma, who seemed to be trying to melt into her chair. Eden was following the conversation with what seemed to be cautious interest, but a flutter of pulse at her throat betrayed her anxiety.

"Of course, the project is very close to my heart, and I hope by it to leave a mark on this city such as no one has done before. I never thought to have my own household divided down the middle by it"—he paused to pierce Eden and Emma with those incredible eyes—"but make no mistake, it will happen."

He took an appreciative sip of his champagne and set the glass down carefully before turning his attention back to Jackie. "May I take it by your presence at that meeting that you yourself oppose the idea of Market Place?" he inquired, spearing a stalk of young asparagus with a tiny fork and releasing it on his plate.

Jay and Eden looked uncomfortable at the turn the conversation had taken—Emma looked nothing short of mortified. Ada cleaved a whipped-butter rose and spread half of it onto a croissant, taking a moment to look up at Jackie as though she could not be more than marginally curious about her answer.

"It's a beautiful building," said Jackie, nodding in Jay's direction, "but I'm not sure why it's needed, and to tell you the truth it doesn't really seem to fit in all that well with its surroundings."

Felix made an almost imperceptible motion of his head that seemed to invite her to continue, though he made no reply.

Jackie went on. "I guess what I'm trying to say is that the Market District has its own look—its own unique personality—and that in my opinion Market Place isn't suited to that personality." There. She had said it. And how angry could he get, anyhow? He was the one who had asked her opinion, after all.

"You may be right about that, Ms. Walsh," said Felix, nodding thoughtfully. "Market Place doesn't look anything like the neighborhood it's going to be built into. It doesn't fit in—on that point you are absolutely correct, and I've always known it to be so. I turned down several of Jay's designs that were considerably more harmonious with their surroundings."

Jay stared at Felix in frank surprise. He had mentioned to Jackie the day they had met that Felix had rejected his previous designs, but evidently Felix's reasoning on the subject was news to him.

"However," Felix continued, "it's possible that the solution in this particular case is not to get rid of Market Place, which I assure you would be impossible in any case with the kind of support I have on the City Council, but to go right to the real core of the matter, and get rid of the neighborhood."

CHAPTER 14

"Mr. Cockrill, there's a Mr. Hahn on the telephone, and he insists on speaking with you." Mona leaned over Felix's shoulder to deliver this message, but it could be heard quite clearly at Jackie's end of the table. The interruption came before Jackie could react to Felix's comment, and it was just as well, she realized. If she'd been able to respond right away, she probably would have regretted it.

Felix Cockrill's revelation of what he obviously intended to do to the Market District was a shock, not just to Jackie but to Jay and Eden and Emma as well. They stared at Felix as though he had just announced plans to murder someone.

Ada took a dainty bite of her croissant, apparently not in the least surprised by her husband's notion of making downtown Palmer over in his own image. Felix himself, who had looked tremendously satisfied when he first spoke, now wore a deep and somewhat frightening frown.

The maid carried a telephone, ready to plug in if her employer was inclined to have the conversation right here in the dining room. She waited patiently while Felix, still frowning, made up his mind.

"I'll take that in the parlor, Mona," he instructed. Mona went out through the double doors, and Felix followed after folding his linen napkin with excruciating care and excusing himself to the assembled company. "This won't take a minute," he assured them, and his tone of voice made

Jackie grateful it wasn't her on the other end of that phone
line.

"Who's Mr. Hahn?" Eden wondered aloud when her
father had left the room.

"He's a business associate of your father's," Ada informed her.

"That's silly, Mother," said Eden. "I know all of Father's business associates quite well, and none of them are
named Mr. Hahn."

"Well, this is one you haven't met," said her mother,
giving her an icy glare.

Eden raised an eyebrow at her uncle Jay, who shook his
head and shrugged. "Nope," he told her, "I've never heard
of him, either."

"I believe he's a contractor," said Ada.

"Well, whoever he is, I wish he hadn't called during
brunch," said Eden. "We see so little of Daddy during the
week as it is."

"Please, everyone," Ada urged. "Don't wait for Felix.
You know how he can be about business."

To Jackie she added, "My husband is a bit single-
minded at times, but it's the secret of his success. He's built
his businesses up from humble beginnings over the past
fifty years with just that sort of determination. I've come
to think of it as one of his most admirable qualities."

"Well, he's certainly been successful," said Jackie, hoping that was a neutral enough comment to disguise her true
feelings about Felix's blind ambition.

"He certainly has," Ada agreed. "Of course there have
been moments we wished he had spent more time with the
family, but we certainly can't deny the results. All his enterprises have prospered."

Ada's face wore an animated smile, but her eyes kept
slipping sideways to the doorway as the voice from the next
room, unintelligibly quiet at first, began to rise in volume.
Ada opened her mouth as if she might make another bit of
polite conversation with which to cover it up, but Felix's
next words were impossible to drown out.

"Goddammit, Ivan, I said turn up the heat, not commit

aggravated assault! The continuation of our relationship depends on your ability to take orders, and so far you haven't shown a lot of promise in that area. This is the last time I want to have to warn you about this, do you understand?''

There was the unmistakable sound of a phone being slammed down into its cradle, and a moment later Felix reappeared in the dining room doorway and took his place at the head of the table, shaking out his napkin again and gracing everyone with a smile. ''Come on, everyone,'' he boomed, a bit too loud and cheerful to be believable to Jackie. ''Let's eat!''

There were a few minutes of near-silence except for requests to pass a particular dish, as everyone at the table filled their plates with food, and kept their private thoughts private. Jackie was grateful they were serving themselves— she had half-feared the white-coated servants would be standing around the table waiting to serve her, and she had more than half-feared she would commit some grave breach of etiquette that would have Ada Cockrill fainting dead away.

The mood at the table was still tense at best, but at least it was gratifyingly informal once the servants had taken the excess serving hardware and gone back into the door in the paneling that led to the kitchen. Jackie allowed herself to hope that the worst of the Cockrill family crises for this meal were over.

''Mother, I've signed up for a volunteer position,'' said Eden, breaking the brief silence.

''That's wonderful, darling,'' Ada beamed. ''I told Greta Thornberry you were just what she needed for the Palmer Ladies' Club charity drive.'' She cut a slice from a salmon fillet. ''I'm so glad you decided to give them some time this year. I've been entirely too busy, I'm afraid.''

''It's not exactly the Palmer Ladies' Club,'' said Eden. ''I talked to Laura Santillo Friday night at the meeting, and I'm going to be working one evening a week at the Women's Shelter downtown.''

Ada put down her fork. ''The Women's Shelter? Where the homeless people stay?'' She managed to put a coloration on the word "homeless" that would have been right at home on far less polite words that she probably never uttered, even in private.

"That's right. They're really short-handed right now, and they've been trying to get some of the students at R.U. to take an interest."

"But why you, dear?" her mother inquired, clearly puzzled at Eden's interest.

"You shouldn't go down there," Emma said, her previous disinclination to talk seeming to have been startled right out of her by Eden's pronouncement. "It's not safe. Mother, say you won't allow it."

"I'm twenty years old, Em," said Eden gently, but with determination. "It doesn't matter what Mother allows or doesn't allow."

"It's an awful place," Emma insisted, "full of awful people. You really mustn't."

"Em's just upset because of the woman who tried to talk to me," said Eden.

That shut Emma right up. Her head withdrew to its former position between her shoulder blades, and she stared at her plate as though something on it had horrified her beyond the capacity for speech.

No one spoke for a moment, then Jay said, "Sounds like a good idea to me, kiddo."

Ada gave him a withering look, but said nothing further. She looked at her husband as if for support, but Felix seemed strangely preoccupied with other thoughts, and had no comment other than "Hmmmm."

"I guess that settles it, then," said Eden. "Would anyone like more of the Saffron Tomatoes?"

As good as the food and the service had been, Jackie was relieved when the servers emerged from the door in the paneled wall with a fresh-baked Dutch Baby rising over the sides of its pan like a big, puffy, golden mushroom of pastry, and a bowl of fresh strawberries and kiwi fruit to spoon into the center.

Jackie was grateful she hadn't been the one to pay for

fresh kiwi fruit in Ohio in October, but she was more grateful to be on the receiving end of the Cockrills' generous grocery budget. One last dish and a polite cup of coffee, and this charming little family party would be breaking up. She couldn't wait to get home to her own relatively normal relatives, black sheep and all, but first she would allow Emma to show her the high points of the Cockrill mansion.

Eden had decided to take her uncle Jay to a movie to alleviate his sad mood. "It's girlfriend trouble," she told Jackie after they had left the table and Jay had gone to get their coats. "He and Gillian Zane were quite a hot item before this whole Market Place issue came between them."

She turned and looked back through the door that led to the dining room. "I wish I hadn't have upset poor Em so," she said, "but it was going to come out sooner or later that I was going to be working at the Women's Shelter. I decided that on top of all the excitement about the Sunday paper, it might go very nearly unnoticed."

"I wouldn't have imagined she'd be quite that unhappy about it," said Jackie, "but then I really don't know Emma that well."

"It's just that she was startled recently when a homeless woman tried to talk to me while we were at the Market. I imagine she was only going to ask me for money, but Em got it into her head that I was being attacked, and dragged me out of there before she could say anything at all. I think the whole idea of poverty and homelessness frightens her to death."

Emma appeared from the doorway to the parlor. "I hope you're not going out without a coat," she said to Eden. "It's going to get quite cool when the sun goes down, you know."

"I know, dear," Eden assured her. "Uncle Jay's going to get my coat right now."

"I wouldn't want you to take ill," Emma told her. "These fall days can be deceptive, and you're forever forgetting to bundle up."

"I'll be fine, Emma." Eden patted the older woman's

arm in a reassuring gesture. "You're always fussing over me."

She turned back to Jackie. "If you get a chance, it couldn't hurt to put in a good word with Gillian," she suggested. "I think she'd pay attention to the right suggestion if it came from you."

"I'm not sure I carry that much weight with Gillian," Jackie told her, "and I'm not so sure a suggestion would be enough after the way she acted toward him Friday night after the meeting."

"Oh, that's why he's been acting like a whipped puppy all weekend," said Eden, shaking her head sorrowfully. "Well, there's a Charlie Chaplin triple feature at the Sofia, and if I can get him laughing, maybe he won't throw himself off the Ohio Street Bridge."

"Oh, I saw that last week!" Jackie told her. "That tight-rope-walking bit in *The Circus* is one of the funniest scenes ever shot," said Jackie. "He won't be able to help laughing."

"Is that the one with the monkeys?" Eden asked. "I think I saw it when I was a child."

"That's the one," Jackie assured her.

"What's this about monkeys?" Jay asked as he came into the foyer carrying Eden's coat. "Are we discussing my niece's boyfriends again?"

"You'll see," said Eden, giving Jackie a wink. "And don't forget that good word," she whispered as she walked past her and out the door.

"I won't," Jackie promised. And she wouldn't forget, but she sincerely hoped Eden wasn't pinning too much on the outcome.

Emma waved goodbye to Jay and Eden, then closed the door behind them. "Would you like to see the house now?" she inquired.

"Lead on," said Jackie.

Emma showed Jackie through a dozen rooms full of expensive furniture and accessories and artwork. She had come out of her shell a little since they left the dining room, and her overpowering family, behind.

The wonderful contemporary and antique pieces from around the world had been collected by Emma's parents and grandparents in their travels over the years, and many came with stories that featured her father and mother in starring roles. Emma told these stories animatedly, as if the protagonists were not her unloving and unlovable parents, but two glamorous and far-off people she had never actually met, but only heard about.

She seemed particularly knowledgeable about the paintings and sculptures that graced her parents' mansion. It was obvious to Jackie that she related more comfortably to them than to the mansion's actual inhabitants, but these were things, after all. They hadn't the same power to intimidate. She showed a great deal of expertise in the arts in general, Jackie noticed.

"You must have studied Art History in college," she guessed.

"A bit," Emma admitted. "I wanted to major, and possibly teach Art, but Father insisted I learn business." She smiled apologetically. "He hadn't yet learned I'm hopeless at business. Actually," she said, patting her pale hair and gazing off in a distracted sort of way, "I'm hopeless at just about everything."

"I don't suppose you went to Rodgers," Jackie said, hoping to change the subject from Emma's shortcomings, which she imagined were the subject of many conversations in the Cockrill house.

"No, we went back east," said Emma.

"We?"

"Ella and I. My sister."

Jackie opened her mouth to respond, but before she could get a word out, Emma took her sleeve and led her out of Ada's study full of Chinese antiques and precious scroll paintings. Twenty feet down the oriental-carpeted hall, she opened the door to a small room furnished in dark woods, with tiny blue flowers on the white bedspread and curtains and matching wallpaper.

"I'll show you," she said. She crossed the room and bent down to open the bottom drawer of a heavy mahogany dresser. "You mustn't tell Mother or Father that I mentioned Ella. Do you promise?" She looked back over her shoulder as if to secure Jackie's word before progressing further.

Jackie was struck, not for the first time, by the notion that underneath her prim, middle-aged exterior Emma Cockrill was still nothing more than a small, frightened child.

"I won't," she promised, feeling as though she ought to be crossing her heart and spitting on the ground. "Not a word."

Emma dug into the deep drawer, which seemed to be filled with old, worn-out clothing. She reached under the old clothes and retrieved something large and flat. When she straightened up again she was holding a leather-bound photograph album with gold leaf scrollwork and lettering on the cover that said "Ella & Emma." She sat down on the blue and white bedspread and patted the space beside her. Jackie sat down gingerly on the side of the bed as Emma opened the album.

The first two pages held a dozen photographs of two identical blond toddlers in various portrait poses. "You have a twin!" Jackie exclaimed. "How wonderful!"

Emma looked at her, and her pale blue eyes refused to give away any expression. "She's been dead for twenty years."

CHAPTER 15

By the time Jackie pulled away from the great circular driveway in front of the Cockrill mansion, she wanted nothing so much as to go home and tell Peter how much she loved him, then call up her mother and tell her the same thing. As it happened, Peter was spending the day at his friend Isaac's house, and her mother was visiting a sick friend in Zanesville. Even Tom and Grania were away for the day, buying supplies in Columbus. In the end, the only available family she could reach was Jake, so she made a slight detour to her apartment and picked him up.

"We've got a couple of places to visit, Jake," Jackie told the big Shepherd as she joined him in the back yard of the condo on Isabella Lane. "Are you ready to go take a walk around town?"

Jake understood the words "go" and "walk," Jackie knew. They were among his favorite words, right behind "eat." He showed that understanding now as he made a beeline for the kitchen door and stood there, tail wagging eagerly back and forth, waiting for her to open it for him. When she did, he trotted inside, unhooked his lead from the hook by the door, and stood waiting for her to clip it onto his collar.

"Hang on, boy," she told him. "I've got to change out of these clothes and re-enter the real world."

Jackie longed to change all the way back from Sunday

Brunch to Sunday Grunge, but in the end she settled for something in between, putting on a nubby tweed blazer over a dark green turtleneck and a respectable pair of jeans. It was nearly a mile from her place to the Market District, but she felt like walking. If there was one thing she needed right now, it was a great big dose of fresh air.

"You know, Jake," Jackie told him as they set out down the former alleyway and out onto the quiet Sunday sidewalks of downtown Palmer, "my family may be getting less respectable by the minute, but I wouldn't trade a one of them—even those wild-eyed Irish revolutionaries—for anybody else's." She patted his shoulder. "And that includes you, big guy."

Jake opened his mouth in a Shepherd grin, tongue lolling. Apparently, he agreed.

Emma had kept Jackie up in that little room for another hour after Jay and Eden had left, showing her pictures and telling her stories about her dead sister, and in the process revealing even more of the twisted dynamics of the Cockrill family.

Ella, it seemed to Jackie as she listened to Emma's retelling of their childhood, had gotten the lion's share of the courage and outspokenness that might ordinarily have been divided between the two sisters, along with a far greater proportion of their father's love and respect. Felix Cockrill hadn't had much use for Emma even as a child, but Ella had been her father's darling, destined for great things in the various Cockrill business enterprises, and just possibly an advantageous marriage to the scion of some very old and very rich midwestern family.

Ada didn't seem to care for either of the twins except inasmuch as she could redesign them the way she did her garden. In fact, she seemed to prefer Emma to some extent, because she was outwardly more malleable, and more willing to be her mother's creature. She battled constantly with Ella, never able to bend her to her will, or change her naturally exuberant personality into one better suited to her notions of what a young woman ought to be.

"Ella was the brave one," Emma told her. "I could never even attempt some of the outrageous things she did. I certainly never could have defied Mother the way she did all her life. All I could do was stand back and watch. Sometimes that was almost as good as doing those things myself."

Emma's expression seemed to indicate that it hadn't been nearly as satisfying as she let on always to play second banana to her more courageous sister. Her words were admiring, but there was more resentment than admiration lurking behind her otherwise bland expression when she spoke of her dead twin.

Ella Cockrill had gone through her twenty years of life frustrating her mother and delighting her father. As Emma had grown quieter, Ella had grown bolder. There was something else, though—something that came through in the photographs of the two girls rather than in Emma's telling of the stories, and it was a great deal more disturbing.

Jackie had paged through the album slowly as she listened to Emma's abbreviated version of the family history. She watched the two chubby blonde toddlers become little girls, and bigger girls, usually posed in some photographer's studio, but occasionally captured in a snapshot in one of their parents' gardens or at a family social gathering. Their facial features continued to be remarkably similar, but their inner differences became clearer with every passing year.

As the twins moved through their teens, they seemed to become one another's opposite in every way except the obvious fact of their resemblance. As the fire slowly died in Emma's eyes, the boldness in Ella's gave way to a sharp-edged glitter that seemed to speak of a growing emotional instability.

Their body language was revealing, too. As Emma grew more hunched and withdrawn, seeming almost to shrink in size, Ella's posture grew increasingly tense, her smile more forced, with every passing year. From the photographic evidence, matters got even worse when the girls went off to college back east.

Emma stopped on the last page of the album and ran her fingers over the last picture of the two of them together. "It was during our second year of college," she said softly, "that Ella committed suicide."

The lunch menu at All Saints Rescue Mission was a great deal more modest than the one at the Cockrill mansion had been, Jackie noted, reading the typewritten sheet tacked up to a square wooden pillar that supported a sagging overhang. Meat loaf, mashed potatoes and gravy, lima beans, fruit cocktail, whole wheat bread. Not exactly gourmet fare, but probably quite welcome anyway on an empty stomach with a hard midwestern winter only a few weeks away.

Jackie tried to remember the last time she had missed a meal. Other than times that had been entirely under her control, she couldn't. Not a single one. It was probably the same for most people she knew, but as she looked up and down the street only half a block from where a homeless woman had died in a trash container in an alley on a cold October night, she knew she was entering a different world here from the comfortable one she and her family and friends lived in.

A cool wind came up and whipped the note around, threatening to rip it from the plastic push-pin and send it flying into the street to advertise All Saints' free lunch far and wide. Jackie pulled her jacket closer and stepped up to the door, Jake following obediently but alertly at her heels.

The old glass-and-wood door was suffering from about a dozen too many coats of badly applied paint, and a crack running through the window in the upper half had been repaired with duct tape. *All Saints Rescue Mission* was painted on the door in no-nonsense black letters. *All Are Welcome.* "I guess that means us, Jake," said Jackie, and pushed open the door.

The front area of the old storefront that was home to All Saints was drab but clean, laboring under as many coats of paint as the outside of the building, with chipped linoleum tile and folding chairs lined up along the walls. Several men sat in the chairs, reading magazines or just staring out the window to the street beyond.

The men looked at Jackie and Jake as they walked past, then looked away again. Jake stayed on his best behavior, eyes, ears, and nose on alert in this strange place, but with the usual air of quiet aloofness he wore around strangers.

A middle-aged woman in a faded shirt occupied the chair behind a battered desk. "Can I help you?" she inquired.

"I'm looking for George Venable," Jackie told her. "Is he here today?"

"He's here every day," she said with a good-natured laugh. "Right now he's in the dining room. Right through there." The woman pointed through a doorway on her right. "Go right on in. That's a very beautiful dog," she added, nodding at Jake.

"Say thank you, Jake," Jackie prompted him.

Jake barked twice in quick succession, and wagged his tail. Peter had taught him that one, and was quite proud of it.

The large dining room was sunny and surprisingly cheerful. Yellow paint had been applied to the walls, and over that a cheery mural painting of downtown Palmer stretched the entire circumference of the room, showing All Saints, the railroad tracks, and a dozen downtown landmarks, including the old clock tower on Terminal Avenue, and Farmers' and Growers' Market. A row of tall windows flooded the walls and floor with light, and the stainless steel surfaces of the serving counter and the kitchen beyond gleamed.

Long folding tables that had seen much better days took up most of the space in the dining room. Benches and chairs that appeared to have been scrounged from a dozen different sources were upended on the tables, and people with mops and brooms were attacking the worn linoleum floor tiles as though their lives depended on it. Jackie could see George Venable's back at the far end of the room.

"Somebody here, George," said one of the mop-wielding men, and George Venable turned to face Jackie.

She gasped. "Oh, my gosh, what happened to you?"

George regarded her from a face full of bruises and bandages as he walked toward her. "It's Jackie, isn't it?"

"That's right. We met at the Market meeting Friday night."

"I remember. How's your mom?"

"A lot better off than you are, would be my guess. What happened?" She pointed to his face, as though she needed to specify what was all too obvious.

"Oh, a couple of guys mistook my head for a soccer ball," said George, feeling a large white gauze bandage gingerly with the tips of his fingers. "And who's this?" He reached out a hand to Jake, who gave it a brief sniff and wagged his bushy tail.

"This is Jake," said Jackie. "We were walking around downtown and thought we'd drop in." In fact, Jackie had known where she was heading since she left her apartment with Jake at heel, but she wanted the visit to seem a bit more social. She had no official capacity to perform here, just feelings she wanted to act upon—facts she wanted to clarify before she felt she could put the matter of Rosie Canty to rest in her mind.

"How do you do, Jake?" said George, which was Jake's cue to hold up his right paw for a handshake. Peter's training was paying off again—Jake's early education had been on matters more serious than doggie etiquette, but now that he was a pet, he could afford to diversify just a bit.

George and Jake shook hands solemnly. "Come on into my office," George said to Jackie. "Can I get you some coffee?"

"Sure." She followed him into a small office off the dining room, which was almost entirely taken up by a battered wooden desk, a guest chair, and several bookcases groaning under the weight of more books by far than they were designed to hold. He motioned her to a guest chair and poured two thick ceramic mugs of coffee.

"Cream and sugar?"

"Black's fine, thanks." Jackie took a seat and Jake lay down by her feet, ears at attention.

George handed her mug over the desk and sat down with a deep sigh of pain and fatigue. "So you want to know how come I look like the poster boy for Palmer Memorial Emergency Room, huh?''

"Only if you feel like telling it," said Jackie. "I realize you must have had to repeat it a dozen times already."

"At least," said George, trying a smile and seeming to think better of it. There were probably stitches under some of those bandages, Jackie thought. She winced involuntarily.

"There's a man named Eugene Seybold who works for me here," George began.

"I know Eugene," Jackie told him. "In fact that's one reason I came today, I confess. I was hoping I could find him here."

George looked surprised. "Well, Eugene's over in Palmer Memorial today. He got the worst of the trouble that happened last night."

"Oh no!" Jackie exclaimed. "Is he going to be all right?"

"He's in pretty good condition," George assured her. "Serious, but stable, is how I think they put it. He'll probably be out of there in a week or so." He doctored his coffee and took a sip to test the results.

"Anyhow, Eugene and I were out looking for one of my off-and-on clients, a man by the name of Bobby Jones. Somebody thought he might be sick and need a place to stay the night. While we were walking down by Fourth and Terminal, these two guys jumped us and pulled us into an alleyway."

"Did you get a good look at them? Could you see who they were?" Jackie asked him.

George shook his head. "There wasn't any light back in there—I think the nearest streetlight was out, and you know how it is over there on Terminal—all closed down and dark after five, anyhow."

"Can you remember anything about them at all?" Jackie asked. Before he could answer, she shook her head. "I'm sorry. You've already been through all this with the police, of course."

"Yeah, I have," said George. "Lieutenant Stillman and

Sergeant Youngquist. But I understand you're a detective of sorts, yourself.''

"Don't believe everything my mother tells you," Jackie warned him. "She's always had an overactive imagination."

"Well, I don't have a problem with telling you, too," he said. "Maybe three heads are better than two when it comes to something like this. I don't mind telling you what I remember." George leaned back in his chair. "I know one of them was tall and skinny, and he had a mustache."

He stared at the ceiling for a few moments, then shook his head. "I can't remember a whole lot of what happened last night, if you really want to know. It's all a kind of jumble, and I'm afraid they put my lights out pretty quick.

" 'Course I'm not much of a fighter," he said apologetically. "Eugene gave damn near as good as he got right at the first. I think that's why they probably just kept on kicking him once they finally got him down. Maybe they just wanted to scare us at first, but I think he may have hurt one of them, and they decided to have their revenge."

Jackie recalled Eugene's powerful and somewhat frightening presence when they had met in the alley out back of. this building only a couple of days ago. "Yeah, I noticed that Eugene looks like he could take pretty good care of himself in a fair fight," she commented.

George nodded. "He used to be a boxer. When they came after us last night and started punching us and kicking us—well, a lot of guys would've run, or tried to. Eugene ripped right into them, trying to protect me. He's a pretty tough old guy," said George fondly. "But I'm afraid years of drinking and living on the street have taken their toll on him. He's not as old as he looks, you know, but this life ages a person beyond their years. He's just not that strong anymore."

"Did either of the men call the other by name?" Jackie asked.

"Not that I recall," he replied. "I don't remember hearing their voices at all." He spread his hands in a gesture of helplessness. "Hey, I know this isn't much help."

Jackie thought for a minute, taking a long sip of her coffee. "You know, this stuff isn't half bad," she commented.

George laughed. "You were expecting dishwater, I imagine. The Coffee Merchant in Farmers' and Growers' donates twenty pounds of coffee beans every month. On Sundays we have the good stuff around here, and Mondays too, if it lasts that long."

Jackie remembered something George had said earlier. "You said you thought maybe the two men were only trying to scare you. Why did you think that?"

"Well, they didn't ask us for money, or say anything else that would give away another motive," said George. "There've been gangs coming down here and beating up on people as long as I've been in charge of this place. A case of simple harassment is what it seems like to me. But attacks of that kind have been increasing around here lately."

"Laura Santillo said something like that," Jackie recalled, "when I talked to her at the Save the Market meeting. Something about a lot of attacks on homeless people. How long has this been going on?"

"Well, there's always been a certain amount of it," said George sadly. "There are always some people looking to bully someone weaker than they are—that's just a sad fact of human nature. But I'd say in the last couple of weeks it's gotten worse. Lots worse."

"I wonder what that time frame means," Jackie mused. "It's not likely to be a coincidence, you know. Did anything happen in the neighborhood around two weeks ago that might have changed things?"

"I don't know if this is connected," said George, "but that's when all this trouble started over Farmers' and Growers', isn't it? Wasn't that about when they announced the Market Place project?"

Jackie remembered the conversation she had overheard earlier that day between Felix Cockrill and his "contractor." "You just may have something there," she said.

CHAPTER 16

"A lot of people around here knew Rosie Canty at least slightly," said Laura Santillo as she led Jackie through the halls of the old girls' school on South Iowa Street that now served as the Downtown Women's Shelter. "But I don't think anyone really knew her well. There's a woman named Alice Roosevelt—one of our off-and-on clients—and I think she and Rosie were pretty good friends most of the time."

"How about the other times?" Jackie inquired.

"Well, neither of them is exactly stable, and they'd get on each other's nerves sometimes. Alice has her pet delusion, of course, and Rosie used to claim she was worth millions, and they'd snipe at one another about that, but there was a genuine friendship under all that, I think."

"Too bad all our friends aren't so easygoing about our delusions," Jackie commented.

Laura laughed. "For sure. Alice has a real thing for her possessions, and when she'd lose something she'd usually accuse Rosie of taking it. Then when the lost item showed up later, or when Alice forgot about it, they'd make up again. It never came down to blows with them as far as I know, although Alice has a history of violence when she gets worked up."

"Is her name really Alice Roosevelt?"

"Someone told me her real name is Rossovich, but she's

got it in her mind that her father's the President. That's Teddy, of course. She acts like a spoiled rich girl, and collects really awful costume jewelry that other people have thrown out, and tells everyone it's worth a fortune. Most of the women around here put up with her pretty well, but a few can be cruel.''

They left the narrow hallway lined with tiny bedrooms behind and emerged into a large common room divided into several sitting areas with old sofas and chairs and bookcases and children's toys. Women of all ages were reading, studying, tending children, and relaxing. One area surrounded a television set tuned to an old black-and-white movie.

Jackie recognized the film they were watching: *Bringing Up Baby*. She had a real thing for screwball romantic comedies—Hepburn and Tracy, Hepburn and Grant, Roz Russell and anybody. Someday she'd have to figure out how to get the University administration to allow her to teach a course in the genre.

"Is Alice in here?" Jackie asked, looking around at the women in the room, trying to spot which of them might be a raving lunatic. They certainly all looked normal enough.

"If she's here today she'll probably be in the transient dorm," said Laura. "It's through there." She pointed to a door at the opposite end of the room.

Before they could cross the room, several small children spotted Jake and surrounded him in the blink of an eye. "What kind of dog is this?" one little boy asked. Before Jackie could answer, the little girl next to him said, "Don't you know anything, you silly? He's a *pleece* dog!''

"He's a German Shepherd," Jackie told them. "And he used to be a police dog, but he's retired now."

"Does that mean he's old? My grandpa retired, and he was *real* old."

"Well, he's pretty old for a German Shepherd," said Jackie, "but he's still young enough to enjoy his retirement."

"Will he bite me?" a wide-eyed three-year-old wanted to know.

"Nope." Jackie hunkered down to be on the kids' level. "He's a big softy. He even has a kitten at home. Or maybe I should say the kitten has him." She held out her hand to the boy who had asked the question. "Here. He'll let you pet him—watch."

She guided the little hand to Jake's head and the boy patted him between his huge black ears. Jake looked over at Jackie as if to ask how long he had to put up with this. "Be brave, Jake," she told him. "They're lots smaller than you are."

When all the children in the room had had a chance to pet Jake and ask questions about police dogs, Jackie and Laura made their escape with Jake in tow. "Bye, Police Dog!" the kids called. "Bye!"

Jake let out a deep sigh.

"I don't think that was too hard on your dignity," Jackie told him. "Stop complaining or I'll put you in there to baby-sit until I leave."

The door opened onto a large dormitory-style room of ancient tubular steel hospital cots made up with military surplus blankets and clean, but worn, linens. A teenage girl with a bucket and a sponge washed a layer of dingy dirt from the inside of one of the big sash windows. A few women sat on one of the beds, having a conversation, but none of them looked to Jackie like she believed she was Teddy Roosevelt's daughter.

Jackie looked at the girl washing windows and wondered if she were homeless, too. She was dressed in a holey tank top and an open flannel shirt over a pair of men's pants several sizes too large for her lanky frame, but Jackie knew that that was the height of fashion lately among teens. Peter and two of his friends had been stopped by the Palmer Police one Saturday afternoon the previous summer on suspicion of vagrancy because of the way they were dressed. They had I.D., so the cop let them go, shaking his head in disbelief.

"Holly's been living here and finishing up high school at Palmer High," said Laura, indicating the young girl. "She did really well on her SATs and she may be able to get some scholarships to attend Rodgers in the spring."

The girl gave them a little wave and went back to her window.

"No sign of Alice in here," said Laura. "But I know a favorite place of hers. Follow me."

They walked down another narrow hall and out a heavy door to the outside. A small gray-haired woman was sitting on the back steps of the building, onto which she had spread a greasy pillowcase that might once have been white, or something close to it.

Several pounds of frankly awful costume jewelry were spread out on the pillowcase, along with half a stick of chewing gum, a nearly empty pint bottle of vodka, a box of kitchen matches, a broken steak knife, and several little cellophane packets of crumbled soda crackers.

There was a sharp scent about her like cheap liquor over stove fuel or cleaning fluid. Jackie wrinkled up her nose in distaste. Jake whuffed a few times, then sat back at the very end of his lead, behind Jackie. Knowing how sensitive his nose was, Jackie could sympathize.

The woman appeared to be matching up earrings into sets, placing like pieces painstakingly in little rows of two all along one side of the rectangle of fabric, and odd pieces on the other side. Bracelets were laid out along the bottom, and necklaces had been wound around a rolled-up newspaper to keep them from tangling. Jackie recognized the headline and photo from Friday's Palmer *Gazette* about the discovery of Rosie Canty's body and the rescue of a small, mixed-breed dog.

"Hi, Alice," said Laura.

"It just never ends, does it?" Alice asked, apropos of nothing Jackie could think of offhand. She looked up at Laura with large brown eyes ringed with thick, dark lashes.

"It certainly doesn't," Laura agreed, obviously unsure of exactly what she was agreeing to.

"It doesn't. You'd think a woman as prominent as I am could get a little break, but no," Alice went on sadly. "No, no, no."

"Your jewelry collection looks terrific," Laura told her.

"Come to my office later and I'll give you some little plastic zipper bags I brought from home for your earrings. Maybe that'll help you keep them a little more organized."

"Yeah," said the woman, "that's a help, all right. It is." She sighed loudly as she ran her grimy hands over the jewelry. "I'd be all right, you know, but I can't keep people's thievin' fingers outta my stuff. Everyone wants my stuff. Every time I count 'em it's different, and Daddy won't like that."

"Whose fingers are you trying to keep out?" Laura asked her. "Is someone stealing your jewelry again? Is it someone at the shelter?"

"It's that Rosie," said Alice, shaking her head. "She never could keep her thievin' fingers outta my stuff. She took one of my poodle earrings night before last. She did, damn her. If she's so damned rich, what does she need with one of my earrings?"

"She gets a little confused about time," Laura explained to Jackie. "Alice, Rosie's dead. She died Wednesday night of the cold. That's why you have to remember to come and get a place to sleep every night until it gets warm again, remember?"

"Yep, she's dead all right," said Alice, "and she still can't keep her fingers off my poodle earrings. She can't." She held up the mate to the missing piece of jewelry, a white-enameled poodle head on gold-toned metal with glittering little glass rubies for eyes. Hell-Poodle. Jackie shuddered.

"I'll bet you just dropped it somewhere," Laura told her. "That's what happened last time, do you remember? It fell out of your pillowcase and you found it again later."

"Who the hell are you?" Alice craned her neck around, seeming to notice Jackie for the first time, and fixed her with a stony glare. "You can't have any of my jewelry. You can't. So just get away. Go on!" She made a shooing motion with one hand.

"I really don't want to take anything from you," Jackie told her. "I was hoping I could ask you some questions."

"Are you from the *New York Times?* The *New York*

Times is always saying bad things about Daddy, so I don't give interviews anymore. I don't.'' She shook her head vigorously, almost dislodging the watch cap perched on top of her dark, graying curls.

"Ms. Walsh isn't a reporter, Alice," said Laura. "And she doesn't want to say anything bad about the President. She just wants to find out some things about Rosie."

"She's a thief!" Alice screeched. Jackie jumped back as Alice lunged at her. "You keep her away from my stuff!"

"Maybe this isn't the best time," Jackie allowed, heart pounding. Alice lit a match on the side of the matchbox and tried to throw it at Jackie's feet.

"Stop that right now!" Laura knocked the match out of Alice's hand and took away the box. "You're not getting these back, either."

"I can get more," said Alice smugly. "There are lots and lots of matches in the White House kitchen, you know. There are."

"I'm sorry," said Laura. "I had no idea she'd be so uncooperative, and as for this. . . ." She held up the box of matches and shook her head, then opened the back door of the shelter.

"It's all right," Jackie said. "Maybe this wasn't such a good idea after all."

"You're no different'n than Rosie," said Alice, "always wanting to take my stuff. You just stay away." She hunched over her pillowcase, bony arms encircling her treasures. "And that goes for your dog, too."

Gillian Zane was helping a customer when Jackie walked into A Readers Market. She waved at Jackie and indicated she'd only be a moment.

"I'm looking for a biography of Sherlock Holmes," said the woman. "Or an autobiography, if you have one of those."

"I'm afraid Sherlock Holmes is a fictional character," Gillian informed her. "I can point you toward some books about him, but they wouldn't be biographies."

"I'm afraid you're wrong," said the customer.

"That's happened a time or two," Gillian admitted. "But the only books I have about Sherlock Holmes are in Literature under Doyle, or the Lit Crit section over in that corner there."

"If you refuse to help me," said the customer in deeply offended tones, "I'll just have to take my business elsewhere."

"Is it okay to bring my dog in here?" Jackie asked after the angry woman had marched out the door.

"You know his manners better than I do," said Gillian. "If it's safe, bring him on in."

"He's very well trained," Jackie assured her. Jake did nothing to counter Jackie's claim, but sat by her left side and looked around calmly at his surroundings.

"He's certainly a beauty," Gillian said, reaching down to give Jake a pat. "So, are you looking for anything in particular?"

"Not really," Jackie said. "I just came by to chat if you have a moment."

Gillian indicated the nearly empty store. "I think my clerk can handle this mob," she said. "I've got an office in the back and I could stand to get off my feet for a few minutes."

She led the way through aisles of bookshelves and past a little reading area with comfy chairs and floor lamps, into a bright little office with a receiving counter along one wall and boxes of books stacked practically everywhere there wasn't either a desk or chairs. "My sanctum sanctorum," she said, allowing Jackie and Jake to pass in front of her and enter.

Jackie took one of the sturdy oak chairs in front of the desk, and Jake lay down quietly at her feet, still showing off those good manners she'd bragged about. "You're a very good boy," she told him, stroking the fur on his back.

"What's on your mind?" Gillian asked as she took a seat behind the desk and plugged in the electric teapot on the file cabinet next to it. "Is it something about Market Place?"

"Sort of," Jackie began, then, "And sort of not. And as if that weren't strange enough, it's also about something that isn't really any of my business. Still with me?"

"I think so." Gillian looked thoughtful, and a little concerned.

"I saw Jay Garnett today."

Jackie expected impatience or even anger when Gillian heard the subject of the conversation, but she only looked sad. "How is he?" she asked.

"Not real good. He's trying not to bother other people with it, but I can tell he's very sad."

"And you're thinking I could do something about that?"

"I don't know," Jackie admitted. "I don't know either of you that well, but I've guessed a little of what's going on, and maybe I shouldn't be interfering—in fact I'm pretty sure I shouldn't be, but I promised someone." She paused for breath, uncertain how to go on. "I just think it's such a shame that two people who care for one another can't get together in spite of a few obstacles."

"A few obstacles is right," said Gillian, leaning back in her chair and closing her eyes. The kettle squealed, and she sat upright again. "Tea?"

"Sure."

"Name your poison." Gillian held out a little wooden tea chest with several kinds of bags.

Jackie picked a Barry's Gold Blend and plunked it into the cup Gillian proffered, a mug that read "Working to support my pet's lifestyle." After buying food for a seventy-pound dog for the past three years, Jackie could certainly identify with that sentiment.

Gillian poured boiling water into both cups and handed Jackie hers. She sat back in her chair again and sighed. "You know, I don't mind that you brought up the thing between Jay and me," she said. "Everyone else has been so careful to butt out that I haven't really had anyone to discuss it with."

Jackie was weak with gratitude that Gillian wasn't offended. ''There's always me,'' she offered. ''I'm an even better listener than I am a meddler.''

''Well, you asked for it,'' said Gillian with a little laugh. ''Our story begins almost six months ago in beautiful downtown Palmer, Ohio.''

CHAPTER 17

Jackie left the bookstore nearly an hour later with three cups of Gold Blend under her belt and a much better feeling than when she had walked in. She had promised Eden she'd put in a good word, and she had. The rest was up to Gillian and Jay.

Maybe it didn't make the greatest logical sense in the world for Jackie to be advising others on the conduct of their romantic lives, seeing as how she was so often confused about her own these days, but she'd have felt terrible if she hadn't even tried to help resolve the conflict between two people with a giant mega-mall standing between them and possible happiness. Jackie couldn't help noticing that her own problems seemed awfully petty sometimes when she could make herself compare them to someone else's.

As she walked with Jake toward home in the dimming autumn afternoon, she thought about the unusual level of involvement she'd been experiencing in other people's business lately, and wondered if it were necessarily a good thing. She had been unable to let go of her near-obsession with a fifty-year-old woman's sad death in the alley behind George Venable's facility for the homeless, and she couldn't help wondering about her motivations there.

Was it only that, like so many others, she had turned away for so long from the growing numbers of people with nowhere to go? Had her recent education on the subject caused her to see nothing but gloom and hopelessness wherever she looked lately? Had her unnerving discovery of Rosie's body caused her to take an unhealthy interest in the subject of her life and death?

And what of the interest she'd taken in Emma Cockrill lately? Emma's problems were about as far removed from those of Rose Canty as Jackie could imagine, yet a case could be made for their strange similarity of circumstances. There was more than one way of being without hope.

Emma had the most luxurious roof in town over her head every night, but she was as clearly as lost as any of the people Laura Santillo and George Venable served every night of the week, every week of the year. In time, some of them would manage to change certain unfortunate circumstances of their lives and make things different for themselves. Would Emma?

Emma might have all the money she needed, but the resources a child must have to grow into a healthy adult had been withheld from her. There were resources an adult required to have a healthy relationship with the world around her that Emma seemed to have no clue how to obtain for herself.

"I guess life is unfair to different people in different ways," Jackie observed to Jake, who cocked an ear toward her as she spoke. "But who ever promised us it would be fair to anybody in any way?"

Jackie paused, but Jake had nothing to say on the subject, as she had feared. "Nobody," she replied, since he wouldn't. "Nobody promised us anything, so if we do have the good fortune to have good people and good circumstances in our lives we shouldn't take it for granted."

Jay Garnett had had the rather mixed fortune to be born with a silver spoon in his mouth and then to have it jerked away by a whim of his father's just before that man's death. According to Gillian Zane, the elder Mr. Garnett had divorced his young second wife, Jay's mother, and cut her and her young son from his will. His first wife was dead, so he had left everything to his only other child, his daughter Ada, who had already inherited her mother's not inconsiderable wealth shortly before her marriage to Felix Cockrill.

Ada had professed to feel terrible about the way things had worked out for Jay, but her concern always stopped somewhere short of actually returning any of his inheritance. She had provided for her brother in the years since their father's death, but there was always a price attached to her generosity.

Jay had been twelve when his father died. The Cockrill lawyers had made certain his mother came away with as little spousal support as could be managed, but Ada had graciously offered to pay his way through college and graduate school. He worked as a graphic artist for a few years, then expressed a desire to study architecture.

Ada had given him the money to attend a prestigious architectural school in California, then influenced Felix to hire him as soon as he had obtained his certificate. He'd been designing buildings exclusively for Cockrill Enterprises ever since. In return, along with the gratitude he felt naturally for all her help, she demanded his unswerving loyalty to Felix and his long-term plan for the future of downtown Palmer, Ohio.

"The sad thing is," Gillian had told Jackie, "Jay doesn't have enough confidence in himself to strike out on his own. And it doesn't help that Ada's always hinting that if he stays on with Felix she'll settle some of his father's money on him."

Apparently Ada was always suitably foggy about how much money she was talking about or when she might let loose of it, but she had been dangling the promise of his lost inheritance over his head like a carrot, while Felix applied the stick in the form of unsavory projects like Market Place. Jay was increasingly frustrated with the arrangement, but also increasingly insecure about his ability to survive out from under the Cockrill umbrella, and reluctant to abandon forever any hope of seeing the money he should already have received from his father's estate.

"Even when he's been certain he could tell Ada where to shove the damned money, he's been afraid of quitting

Felix. It's a sure thing he could never work in Palmer if Felix decided to use his influence to prevent it, and who knows how far that influence might reach?''

Gillian hadn't been entirely unsympathetic about Jay's quandary, but knowing he had been assigned to design the huge commercial/residential complex that was going to doom Farmers' & Growers'—and her bookstore—to destruction was more than she could take.

"When he told me what Felix wanted him to do, I told him he should quit his job," Gillian had informed her over tea in her office.

"And of course he didn't," said Jackie.

"He said he couldn't," Gillian recalled with a sigh. "I said he wouldn't. I guess the truth was somewhere in the middle, but I was too angry to help him find it. I told him it was Market Place or me."

"Have you seen any of his early designs for Market Place?" Jackie asked.

"I wouldn't look at them," Gillian told her. "He did tell me that since he didn't have a choice about whether or not to design the project for Felix, he was trying to create something that would take the place of the old building without betraying the neighborhood around it."

"But that wasn't enough."

Gillian shook her head. "I couldn't live with that as a compromise—not when I knew it meant the death of the Market, and I knew that was entirely unnecessary to anyone but Felix Cockrill. And then Felix rejected those designs anyway, and now we'll have the monstrosity." She had looked up at Jackie then, tears bright in her eyes. "Was I wrong?" she asked. "Do you think I was too obstinate?"

"I think the word I had in mind was 'inflexible,' " said Jackie.

"I think a better one might be 'pig-headed,' " sighed Gillian. She poured Jackie, then herself, the last of the tea, and stirred sugar into hers with a distracted expression.

"But you had to be the one to decide what you could live with," said Jackie. "You've spent years building this business, and you didn't want to lose it. I feel sorry for

Jay, but that doesn't mean he was right and you were wrong.''

"It doesn't exactly mean the opposite, either," Gillian said. "Maybe if we'd talked about it more, a solution would have occurred to us somewhere along the way. But I cut off any hope of that by refusing to discuss it." A tear slipped out of the corner of her eye and down her cheek. She wiped it away angrily with her sleeve. "Jay's the only human being in the Garnett family," said Gillian. "And I couldn't give him credit for that."

"I don't think it's too late to talk," Jackie told her.

"Where did you say he and Eden went?" Gillian asked. "To the Sofia?"

Jackie stood up, pulled Gillian's coat off the rack by the desk, and handed it to her. "If you hurry, you can still catch the tightrope-walking scene in *The Circus*," she told her.

"So as usual, I'm chock full of good advice for others," she said to Jake as they walked up the steps to their front door, "and still as confused as ever when it comes to my own life."

She opened the door and unclipped Jake's lead from his collar. Charlie, who had been curled up in a fuzzy ginger ball in Jackie's favorite reading chair waiting for his playmate to return, unwound and launched himself onto Jake's broad back as soon as the big Shepherd came within range.

Jake began his usual galumphing gallop around the front room, designed to dislodge the feline rider so that Jake could settle down to have his head chewed on for a few minutes before submitting to a good ear cleaning. It was a routine they both knew well. Unfortunately, so did Jackie. "Watch it, guys!" she cautioned.

As Jake rounded a corner his claws slipped on the polished hardwood floor and he went sliding sideways into a Parsons table. Charlie jumped ship (or dog) as the table tottered toward them, and Jackie arrived at the scene in time to right the table and save the Beleek teapot that sat on it. Trembling, she cradled the delicate Parian China pot in both arms and tried to catch her breath. The teapot, a pale basket-weave pattern with delicate, hand-painted shamrocks, had been brought back from County Tyrone on a visit her parents had made to Ireland before she was born. It was high time to find a safer place for it.

"All right, let's take this game outside, gentlemen!" Jackie said. Crossing to the kitchen where she set the endangered teapot on a countertop, she opened the door that led to the back yard, and the two of them trotted obediently outside.

"Come back when you're tired enough to lie down for a while," she called after them, and shut the door. Having Charlie around had made Jake feel like a puppy again, but between them they were taking years off her life.

The phone rang. Jackie glanced at the caller ID field that normally told her who she'd be talking to, but this person had blocked their number. Jackie was occasionally pestered by heavy breathers, but they tended to call late at night, and it was barely dinner time. Sighing, she picked up the receiver. "Hello?"

"Jackie? It's Cooper. Is Peter around?"

Jackie thought of all the sarcastic things she wanted to say to the man who almost never called his son, seldom arranged to spend time with him, and frequently broke the dates he did make with Peter when anything more promising came along. "He's at a friend's house today," was what she did say. There was no point wasting her breath on Cooper Walsh.

"He left a message on my phone about some school project he wanted help with. Is he having some sort of problem? Is he doing all right in school?"

"He's doing fine, Cooper," Jackie told him. "He needed to get some information about your side of the family for a genealogy project. Why don't you call him back later tonight?"

"I'm afraid I'll be out later tonight," said Jackie's ex-husband. "I've got some important things I've got to do." From the background sounds Jackie could hear behind Cooper, he was already out doing those important things. That, or he had converted his Kingswood condo into a noisy cocktail lounge.

"I'll just bet you do," Jackie muttered under her breath.

"What's that? I can't hear you. Anyhow, if you could tell me what it is he needs to know I could tell you, and then he wouldn't have to wait God knows how long to get the information."

And you won't have to actually talk to him and take the chance he'll ask about spending the weekend with you sometime before Christmas, Jackie thought. Well, her bitterness about Cooper's cavalier attitude toward fatherhood wouldn't get Peter's school assignment finished. She took a calming breath and tried to sound as friendly as the situation seemed to demand. "He needs the names of your parents and all the grandparents and great-grandparents as far back as you can remember."

"Okay," said Cooper thoughtfully.

"Let me get a pen," said Jackie.

Five minutes later she had all the information Peter's father could provide on the spur of the moment. He promised solemnly to call his mother in Cleveland the next day and fill in the remaining blanks. By biting her tongue, Jackie managed not to remind him that he'd promised a lot of things in the past that he hadn't made good on, starting with the promise he made when they were married to be faithful to her.

Oh, well, why quibble, thought Jackie as she hung up the phone. She was a thousand percent better off without Cooper, and she might never have figured that out if it hadn't been for his philandering ways.

She really couldn't imagine herself—the Jackie Walsh she knew now—as a suburban housewife gritting her teeth through more years of meaningless existence, a shallow life among shallow people, because it seemed to be expected of her.

It was almost as if she'd been sleeping through those years with Cooper, and when the wake-up call had come, the true personality she'd carefully buried because Cooper never seemed to care for it had refused to go back to sleep

again. If she'd overlooked Cooper's womanizing and remained married for the sake of form, would she ever have
become herself again? It was more than a little frightening
to think that she might not have.

She marched the note up to Peter's room, and left it on
his desk by the computer. Downstairs, she rummaged
around in the freezer for a no-brainer dinner. When her
hand closed on a plastic bag full of Cannelloni Tre From-
aggio, she knew she'd found it.

CHAPTER 18

"Does the name Ivan Hahn ring a bell?"

"Do I get a good grade if I give you the right answer?"

Jackie reminded herself that being patient with Evan Stillman would get her a lot further than rapping his knuckles with a ruler would, however much she might feel he deserved it. She had come down to the Palmer Police Department early Monday morning before she had to be at Rodgers University for her office hours, hoping she could make Evan fit together some of the pieces that had been rattling around in her mind all the night before, keeping sleep at bay. "I just have a hunch you might have heard the name before, that's all."

Evan motioned at the coffee pot that occupied a little square table near the filing cabinet in his office. Jackie shook her head. Evan poured a mugful for himself and added sugar. "Before I tell you whether I've heard of this guy or not, why don't you tell me why you need to know? You're not still trying to make my life miserable about that accidental death case with the Jane Doe, are you? 'Cause if you are I've got to tell you, Jackie, I don't understand it."

"What is it you don't understand exactly, Evan?" Jackie asked him.

Evan paced from the coffee maker to the coat rack and back again, formulating his reply. "You know, when you and Mike McGowan were a thing for a couple of years, well, that seemed to be the main reason you were always involved in some way with police business. It seemed like a natural outcome of that relationship, although a lot of the time you were a little too involved, if you take my meaning.''

Jackie took Evan's meaning pretty well, but she decided against saying anything at this point. Instead, she nodded her head in what she hoped was an understanding manner.

''It didn't seem to bother Mike,'' Evan went on, ''so I tried to mind my own business about it. I mean, you weren't breaking any laws or anything. So now Mike's in Hollywood writing a TV series, fergodsake.''

At this point Evan rolled his eyes toward the ceiling and sighed. It seemed he didn't get why Michael McGowan would leave a perfectly good job where people shot at him only occasionally, and take off for the land of eternal summer to sit by swimming pools full of scantily clad young women and write television scripts. ''And you've got yourself a new boyfriend—congratulations, by the way, and I don't want to sound unfriendly or anything, but I don't think I understand why you're still poking around in our murder cases.''

Jackie thought for a moment about Evan's use of the phrase ''poking around.'' Was that what she was doing? She was trying to bring some closure to this thing for herself if no one else, but Evan had a way of making it sound so trivial. ''I am in a way, but before you get all exercised about it,'' she put up a hand to ward off Evan's attempted interruption, ''there are some things I think you should know.''

Evan looked at her steadily through lowered brows. ''Such as?''

''Such as there's been an unusual amount of harassment of homeless people in the Market District since the Market Place project was announced. There have been cases of assault, assault and battery. Saturday night two men were beat up pretty badly. One of them is in the hospital right now.''

"We already know about those incidents, Jackie," said Evan wearily. "We're investigating them. That's what we do. That's why we're the police."

"Yeah, and I'm not. I know."

"I never said that." Evan sat back down in his chair.

"Tell me you never thought it."

"I think you know better than that," Evan said, cocking an eyebrow. "I take my job seriously. I'm a trained professional at this job. I don't think an amateur can do it as well as I can. That doesn't mean I don't like you, but it does mean I get concerned when you start acting like a wannabe cop."

"So you want to know why I'm still poking around in your Jane Doe case?"

"Yeah, I do. Partly for professional reasons, I guess, and partly just plain old curiosity."

"Cosmo said the dead woman had a very high blood-alcohol level," she began.

"Up to here," Evan confirmed, gesturing somewhere near his eyebrows.

"Two different people have told me she never drank," Jackie told him. "Apparently she was allergic to alcohol, and suffered terrible headaches if she drank even a little bit."

"That's anecdotal evidence," Evan said. "It doesn't stand up against a good old BAC test, you ought to know that."

"I do know it, but doesn't it seem a little strange to you? And how about the fact that she left her dog outside in the cold? Does that make sense?"

"While you were getting all this information on Jane Doe's allergic reactions to alcohol, did anyone happen to mention that she was bug nuts?" Evan inquired.

"Yes, I know that, but . . ."

"Then as far as I'm concerned, all bets are off," he said. "She wasn't right in the head, Jackie—who knows what she might do? Including drinking too much to keep warm on a freezing night no matter how that might make her feel in the morning. Including forgetting about her dog, for all

I know, or for all you know, either.'' He rubbed the back
of his neck and leaned back a bit. ''Maybe you're just
thinking about all this way too much. Forget about dead
people for a while. Get another hobby.''

''I didn't ask to find that body Thursday morning, you
know,'' she told him.

''Well, I didn't actually think you went around scouting
alleys for corpses,'' Evan told her, ''but damned if you
don't seem to have the damnedest luck about these things!''

''Don't I know it,'' Jackie sighed. ''Honest, Evan, I
don't know what it is that gets me involved in these cases,
but once I am, I just have to keep at it until I know what
happened.''

''Listen, Jackie, I'm not as casual as Mike was about
your involvement in police business. That's just the way I
am. It's nothing personal.''

''Well, thanks for that, anyhow, Evan.''

''And as much as it hurts, I've even got to admit that
you're pretty good at it. And that dog of yours is no slouch,
either.''

Jackie was overwhelmed. ''Gee, thanks, Evan. I mean,
really. I don't think you've ever actually said that to me
before.''

''I know I haven't. And if you tell anyone I did this time,
I'll deny it.''

''Understood. Now what about Ivan Hahn?''

Evan seemed to know when he was whipped. ''He's a
small-time neighborhood operator. Loans, muscle, that sort
of thing.''

''Is anyone looking at him for Saturday night's assault
on Eugene Seybold and Charles Venable?''

Evan shook his head, but the ghost of a smile crossed
his lips. Jackie pretended not to notice.

''Not yet,'' he said, guarded. ''Now I guess I have to
ask why you think we should be.'' He didn't look particularly happy about it, she noted.

''Because I overheard a phone conversation between him
and Felix Cockrill yesterday, and I spent most of last night
thinking about it while I should have been sleeping. It

sounded a lot like Hahn was putting the strong-arm on somebody for Cockrill.'' She recounted the partial conversation she had overheard in the Cockrills' dining room the day before.

"That could have been anybody," Evan said wearily. "Maybe old man Cockrill has a business rival who's giving him nightmares, and he wants Hahn to put the frighteners on the guy for him. It happens. Business and crime aren't all that far apart sometimes. We can't step in until someone crosses the line. You know that."

"Okay, but tell me this—is Ivan Hahn tall and skinny, with a mustache?"

"Oh, come on. In a town this size, hundreds of guys fit that description. Two or three of them work on the Palmer force."

Evan pushed a hand through his thinning hair, and Jackie reminded herself to back off before he started tearing it out in chunks. "I interviewed George Venable," he said patiently. "I got the description of his attacker. I'm not abysmally stupid, you know."

"I know. And I'm sorry. I didn't mean to imply you weren't doing your job."

"But Venable's description of the guy that beat him up isn't enough to go on to arrest Ivan Hahn," Evan continued, "no matter what your famous amateur detective's intuition might tell you."

"I understand that, but listen to me for just a minute, okay?"

"Okay. You got two or three minutes. Don't ever say I don't listen to you."

Now it was Jackie's turn to roll her eyes. "I won't," she promised him. "When I talked to George Venable at All Saints, he said the increase in assaults on homeless people started around the time Cockrill Industries announced their plans to tear down Farmers' and Growers' and build Market Place."

"Let me guess," said Evan. "You think there might be a connection between Cockrill's new supermall and somebody beating up homeless guys."

"Yes," said Jackie. "I do. This is about more than one downtown complex. Felix Cockrill doesn't plan to stop tearing down Palmer when he's got his Mondo Condo up and running. I've got this from the horse's mouth. He wants to rebuild the entire Market District in his own image, and keep right on going from there."

"Distasteful, but hardly illegal," was Evan's comment.

"I think Cockrill's putting out the word to the homeless and the people who are trying to make things better for them that there's no room for them in his new version of the city," Jackie said.

"Okay. You're entitled to your opinion on that, but I've seen nothing that implies that your notion of the facts are actually the facts. And while I'm on a roll reading your mind, let me take it one step further," Evan continued. "You also think there might be a connection between somebody beating up homeless guys and the dead woman in the alley."

Evan had hit the nail on the head. Maybe he knew her better than she had given him credit for. Or maybe she was just that transparent. "It's not entirely far-fetched, is it?"

"It's pretty far out there, Jackie, if you really want to know," Evan told her. "People beat up on homeless guys all the time. When we find them, we arrest them, but we can't find all of them. We do know there's a gang of toughs that's been responsible for other attacks like this, and we're watching them. One of these guys fits George Venable's description of his attacker pretty closely. As a matter of fact, and I presume I can trust you to keep this under your hat, we expect to make a couple of arrests on this case no later than tomorrow night."

"I think these beatings may have a different motive than the desire to hurt someone who can't fight back," Jackie told him.

"I'm not a psychologist," Evan said. "I don't know what makes people do the sick things they do, but I know that whoever's assaulting homeless men in the Market District, Jackie, it isn't Felix Cockrill, and it probably isn't anybody working for Felix Cockrill, either. As for your second wild hair, that Jane Doe wasn't assaulted, she died of too much booze and some hellish cold temperatures.''

"She isn't a Jane Doe anymore," said Jackie. "She has a name. It's Rose Canty.''

"What she doesn't have is an open case with this department,'' said Evan.

"Good," Jackie told him, getting up from her chair. "That means you won't have to get all excited if I decide to investigate her death.''

She was out the door before Evan could come up with a reply.

CHAPTER 19

Jackie had laid out all her facts for Cosmo Gordon, but she could see by his expression, as Palmer's Chief Medical Examiner regarded her across the pile of clutter atop his desk, that it wasn't going to do her a bit of good. He regarded her with a weary look not unlike the ones she had just received from Evan Stillman, and shook his head almost imperceptibly, biting his lower lip for good measure.

She had come here directly from Evan's office in the Palmer Police Department building across the street, to try one last time to get some kind of official action taken on Rosie Canty's death. The alternative was that she would have to dig around in the case herself, and she definitely didn't want to do that until she knew there was no other recourse open to her.

Cosmo had listened a good deal more patiently than Evan had to Jackie's recital of claims that Rosie Canty had been allergic to alcohol and refused to drink for fear of the awful headaches that always followed. He had heard her argument against Rosie having crawled into the dumpster and passed out, leaving Arlo, her constant companion, outside to freeze. He had even refrained from comment as she explained how something about his pat explanation of the woman's death just didn't ring true to her. She was as certain as she could be that he had given every possible consideration to her arguments.

And in the end he had decided she was wrong.

"Autopsies cost the city money," Cosmo explained. "It's not bad enough that I have a minimum staff for the number of post-mortems that have to be done every week in a city this size, but I can't perform another autopsy on your Jane Doe . . ."

"Cosmo . . ."

"I'm sorry, Rose Canty, then. I can't even consider it without being able to justify it to the city, and frankly, Jackie, there's nothing about what you just said to make me feel this one is justified."

"But Cosmo . . ." Jackie began.

Cosmo held up a hand. "You've been investigating crimes off and on for what—three years? I've been determining cause of death for more than thirty. Do you think that was the first time a body has been found in an alley in this city? Do you think we don't come across this sort of thing too damned often?"

"Believe me," Jackie told her friend, "I'm learning every day how little I knew."

"Then trust me on this one. The woman died the way I said she died. I wish I could tell you that was strange or unusual, but I can't. It's just something that happens."

Cosmo reached over the desk and patted Jackie's hand in a fatherly sort of way she didn't really care for, but had learned to put up with. "I know you can't stand not knowing the truth," he told her, "but when you have it, maybe you need to learn to accept it. This time I think you've been going a little too far out on a limb for your answers."

Jackie looked out Cosmo Gordon's office window at the tranquil autumn scene two stories below. Life was humming along as usual on this October Tuesday afternoon in the Palmer, Ohio she and Cosmo and all their friends inhabited, and chances are it always would.

Their familiar and comfortable Palmer had all the things she could see from here—distinguished old buildings and old, spreading oaks, and green-painted park benches and neatly dressed civil servants on their lunch breaks, fattening up the city's squirrels with their leftovers. It had carefully

manicured City Administration Building lawns bordered by
orderly city streets, and well-fed law-abiding citizens moving to and fro on clean, litter-free sidewalks. It wasn't a
half bad place to live, when you came down to it.

Lately, though, Jackie had been spending more and more
time, in her mind and occasionally in body as well, in a
different Palmer—the less comfortable world inhabited by
people like Rosie Canty, Eugene Seybold, and Alice Roosevelt, or Rossovich, whichever. In this darker and colder
world, the small comforts others took for granted, such as
a bed for the night, or a warm meal on a cold day, were
not guaranteed.

In this world, if you put any faith in the opinions of
Eugene Seybold, someone could end your life in a cold
alley and if you were homeless, the people in authority
wouldn't really care. Jackie was beginning to wonder if
Eugene might not have a point after all.

"You're familiar with Occam's Razor, I imagine," said
Cosmo, bringing her back to the moment.

"Yeah," Jackie sighed in spite of her best efforts at self-
control. "Don't go looking for complicated explanations
for something when there's a perfectly good simple explanation that fits the facts."

"I couldn't have said it better myself," he said. "I hope
you won't hold this against me, Jackie. Your friendship
means a lot to me, but if I were to bend rules every time
a friend asked me to . . ."

"It's okay, Cosmo," Jackie told him. "Thanks for listening to me anyway. It was worth a try." She got up from
the guest chair opposite his desk and gathered up her things.
"So you agree with Evan that the case is definitely
closed?"

"Definitely. Until someone comes up with some compelling new evidence. Not feelings," he emphasized. "Evidence."

"I understand. Would I be bending the rules too much
to ask if I could get a look at Rosie Canty's personal effects? I know it's a weird request," she added before
Cosmo could make this observation himself. "It's just that

finding her body was such a strange experience for me. The whole thing has been disturbing my sleep more than a little.''

''That's understandable, I guess,'' Cosmo put in. ''You find a body and you had this idea there might have been foul play. I guess your past experience sort of inclined you toward that conclusion, but now it's turned out to be the wrong one. You probably feel the need for some sort of closure on this whole thing.''

''Yeah,'' Jackie agreed, nodding. She felt just a tad deceitful for leading Cosmo on this way, but damnit, he'd brought it on himself. ''I guess maybe that's it.''

''I don't know if seeing a pocketful of junk is going to help, but I don't have a problem with it,'' he said. ''Let me make a phone call and I'll have the stuff up here in five minutes.'' Cosmo seemed eager to offer Jackie something after closing the door in her face on the autopsy issue. That was fine with her. She wanted some answers to the mystery of Rosie Canty and she'd take help wherever she could get it.

Ten minutes later she was closing up the string tag on the brown kraft paper envelope and handing it back over Cosmo's desk. ''I guess you were right,'' she told him. ''It's just a lot of junk. But it was good of you to go to the trouble. And thanks again for everything, even if I didn't get my way this time.''

''You can always come to me,'' Cosmo told her. ''I may not always agree with your conclusions about things, but I'm always willing to listen.''

Jackie walked toward the office door, then turned back around. ''Seen our buddy Marcella lately?'' she asked as casually as she could manage.

''As a matter of fact we're having dinner tonight,'' said Cosmo just as casually.

''Well, you be sure to tell her hi for me,'' said Jackie.

''I'll do that,'' Cosmo replied.

Jackie took the elevator down to the lobby and walked out into the autumn sunshine. By declaring the case of Rosie Canty's death closed, Evan and Cosmo had given her carte blanche to investigate this thing on her own, as far as she was concerned. And that's just what she was going to do.

Just as soon as she figured out how.

CHAPTER 20

Jackie drove to Rodgers University in a thoughtful sort of daze to put in her Monday morning office hours. She replied automatically to greetings from several students and colleagues as she crossed the campus without actually registering who had spoken to her or what, exactly, they had said.

She let herself into her office, hardly more than a glorified closet, and turned her OUT sign to read IN. She could always hope everyone would stay away, but that never seemed to happen and if a miracle should occur, there were plenty of other things she ought to be doing with the time. When she found herself resenting having to be here today, she reminded herself that a few hours spent listening to students' problems frequently made her forget, at least temporarily, about her own.

Reams of paperwork already put off for far too long were starting to reach for the low ceiling of the little cell she had been granted in the Longacre Communications Center, and what surface should otherwise have been visible on her desk was covered over in little yellow sticky notes reminding her of calls and duties and obligations she really should get around to one of these days. Probably not today, though.

At least her cell had a window, and she opened it up to a blast of cool air and the weakening sunshine of an Ohio autumn. Last week's snowstorm had been just a gentle reminder of things to come. November would bring more snow, and this time there wouldn't be any warm days to follow, or at least not for several more months. Would another frozen man or woman be found in another alley before spring came again?

Without her willing it, her mind went back to Cosmo's office, to the brown paper envelope that had held the contents of the pockets of a dead woman. There had been a length of chain—a dog leash for Arlo—and a tiny pocketknife, red with silver roses engraved on the handle. A few crumpled dollar bills and some loose change were in there—a net worth of less than six dollars.

Among the few remaining items was a torn-out piece of a newspaper article, the first few columns of Marcella Jacobs' first piece on Market Place, carefully folded in four. Rosie had probably been concerned about the possible impact on her already hazardous life of an upscale urban complex appearing in her back yard, and who could blame her?

Not the least of her worries might have been the impact on All Saints and the Downtown Women's Shelter, who depended heavily on donations from Farmers' & Growers' merchants. The local farmers alone donated tons of unsold food every year to help feed the less fortunate. Without those donations, Jackie realized, the future of Palmer's poorest residents looked pretty dim. Without the Farmers' & Growers' Market to hold the Market District together, the future of that entire section of downtown Palmer didn't look much better, unless you happened to be Felix Cockrill, a truly unappetizing prospect.

Jackie was grateful when students dropped by from time to time while she was there and interrupted her dark reverie with their questions—theirs were far easier to answer than her own. When the clock ticked over to 12:00, she closed the window and made her escape. Tom wasn't expecting her to drop by this afternoon, but she knew that wouldn't matter.

• • •

Jackie pulled the Blazer up into the driveway of Cusack Kennels and waved at Joseph, who was putting a frisky young Irish setter through her paces on the patch of lawn in front of the office. Using a short training lead, he walked back and forth with the young dog, reminding her to stay at heel and giving a quick tug when it seemed required to reinforce his commands.

The setter quite obviously wanted to be off up the hill chasing the squirrels that ran up and down the big oak tree, getting their acorn stores laid in for the winter. Jackie could sympathize with the dog's distraction—she'd never been awfully good at obedience herself.

There were plenty of things that needed doing at home, she knew, but she also knew that she had been right to come here first. Tom's company was always good for her. Just the sight of his face was always enough to lift her spirits, and he had a way of bringing matters into perspective, especially on those days when Jackie found her own perspective severely lacking, like today.

She had made a detour past her apartment and collected Jake, who as always was ready for a drive anywhere and loved visiting Tom almost as much as Jackie did. They enjoyed a companionable, one-way conversation on the way over, with Jake demonstrating the expected sympathy with Jackie's views on homelessness and Rosie Canty and the Market Place project and just about anything else. A good listener is hard to find, Jackie thought, but not if you happen to own a dog.

She climbed down from the Blazer and opened the back door. "Your boss making you do all the work again?" she called to Joseph as she held onto Jake's lead and let him jump down onto the gravel driveway.

"Just like always," Joseph said pleasantly. "I'm glad someone understands who really runs this place." He gave her a grin. "That little lost dog of yours has made Cusack Kennels pretty popular," he told her. "Not only has that gorgeous police detective been by every day to see him, but the phone's been ringing off the hook. Seems like everyone in town wants to adopt Arlo.''

"I wish I were so popular," Jackie said, trying to sound more casual than she felt. So Bernie Youngquist was visiting every day, huh? That's what she wanted to hear to make her feel better. Yep. "So where's the lazy bum now?" she inquired. "Taking a nap?"

"Oh, he's in the office, probably goofing off as usual."

"Well, maybe I can catch him at it," said Jackie. "I'll just sneak in the back door."

Jackie walked past the damaged kennel building, where a stack of lumber and cans of paint awaited Tom and Joseph's inclination to repair the relatively minor ravages of Friday night's fire. It wasn't until she walked around the back of the building that housed the grooming facilities and Tom's office that she saw the little white car parked in the smaller driveway next to Tom's house. She recognized it immediately. Her stomach tightened and her heart thumped unhappily.

Just then Tom came out of his office with Bernie Youngquist. He had his arm around her shoulder. Jackie ducked back behind the corner of the building, dragging Jake with her. "Thanks, Tom," Bernie was saying, "I knew I could count on you." Jackie peeked around the wall just in time to see Bernie give Tom a warm hug, then walk to her little car and get in.

Jackie stayed behind the office until she heard Bernie's car pull out of the driveway and onto the highway below. Then she took a deep, shaky breath and came out of her hiding place as though she'd just been casually walking over from the other side.

Tom smiled when he saw her. "You know, I didn't know how much I wanted to see you today until just now," he said, walking up to her and putting his arms around her. "Of course I'd have figured it out eventually."

"Yes, I wanted to see you, too, Jake," he assured the Shepherd, who had been sitting there waiting patiently for his share of Tom's attention. He ruffled the thick fur on

Jake's neck. Jake panted happily and thumped his tail against Jackie's feet.

"I know you weren't expecting me to drop by," Jackie said, trying to keep her voice under control. It wasn't easy. She had been taken by surprise, as always, by how threatened she felt by Bernie Youngquist, and watching her hug Tom hadn't lessened that threat any.

"I love surprises," Tom told her, nuzzling her neck. "Especially when they come from you. Homemade cookies, stray dogs, whatever."

Jackie buried her face in Tom's shoulder and tried to bury her feelings of uncertainty at the same time. Tom seemed to sense her mood. He put a finger under her chin and pulled her face up, frowning slightly.

"Is something wrong, babe?" His deep blue eyes were full of concern.

"I don't know," she said, voice trembling slightly in spite of herself. "You tell me."

Tom seemed to think about this for a long moment before the light dawned. "Ah, I think I see what the problem is," he teased, kissing the end of her nose tenderly. "Your beautiful dark eyes have picked up a peculiar shade of green, my sweet. I guess I ought to be flattered, but I'd rather you didn't feel jealous on my account. You're the only woman for me." He held up two fingers to illustrate his point. "Scout's Honor."

"Am I really?" She searched his eyes for signs of his feelings, and found them.

"Absolutely," he said softly. "That's what I've been trying to tell you for months."

"But . . ." Jackie made a helpless gesture at the spot in Tom's driveway where Bernie's car had been only a minute before.

"That little demonstration of exuberance on Bernie's part that you apparently witnessed," Tom was obviously trying not to smile at Jackie's discomfiture, but the corners of his mouth were twitching just a bit, "was on account of your mutual friend, Arlo." Tom put his arm around Jackie's waist and pulled her along toward the house.

"What about Arlo?" Jackie asked him.

"Bernie's decided to move into a house so she can adopt him," said Tom. "It's going to be a couple of weeks before she can get everything arranged, and she was asking me if I'd board him for her until she gets moved. I had to tell her I didn't want her money—little Arlo's become like part of the family around here, and I'd feel awful charging him rent."

"Joseph told me Arlo had more offers than Tom Cruise," Jackie said.

"He's having his fifteen minutes," Tom agreed. "Lucky for me I didn't have to decide which of all those strangers got to take him home. I think Bernie will be perfect for him."

"Maybe you should have adopted him yourself," Jackie told him. "If you had a ferocious watchdog like Arlo around here, maybe people wouldn't come around and try to burn the place down."

"You could be right," said Tom, opening up the door to the house and pulling her inside. He gave her a wicked grin and kissed her neck like he meant it. "Let's discuss it later."

CHAPTER 21

"The police have closed the case," Jackie told Tom when they were sitting at his kitchen table over cups of coffee and sandwich makings. Jake sat near Jackie's feet by the table.

"Arlo's owner? The homeless woman?" Tom asked as he opened a loaf of seven-grain bread and removed four slices.

Jackie nodded as she took two of the slices from him. "I spent a lot of time trying to convince them, but Cosmo won't consider a new autopsy without some pretty convincing evidence, and unfortunately, neither he nor Evan are that crazy about the evidence I've given them so far." She struggled with the lid on the mustard jar, but it refused to budge.

"You've given them evidence?" he said, raising an eyebrow as he reached out and twisted off the stubborn lid. "How did you get . . . ? Oh, I see." He nodded slowly. "You're still trying to figure this thing out on your own, aren't you?"

Jackie looked at Tom's face. He was trying hard not to let it show, but she knew that face well, and she was sure she saw doubt and uncertainty there.

"I guess it's hard for you to understand why I do this sort of thing," she told him. "It's not that easy for me to understand sometimes either." She reached for a knife and the block of sharp cheddar, partly to distract herself from her emotions.

It was very important to Jackie that she not drive Tom away, but she couldn't hold onto him by pretending to be someone she wasn't. She had tried that once, and it had wasted years of her life. She wouldn't do it again, no matter what.

"I guess I can see how you'd be curious about what happened to that poor woman," said Tom. "I was curious myself. But that's been settled now, hasn't it? They know how she died, and her dog is going to have a good home, and it's over. You can put it to rest and think about more important things." He looked at her carefully. "You can, can't you?"

Jackie started to slice some cheese, but her hands were trembling. She put down the knife.

"Here. Let me do that for you," said Tom. He cut off several slices of cheese, but his hands weren't much steadier than hers. The slices were ragged and comical, but Jackie didn't feel much like laughing. Jake watched the procedure carefully in case any scraps of cheese might find their way onto the floor.

"I wish I could forget about it," she said finally. "But there are still just a whole lot of unanswered questions."

"But aren't those up to the police?" Tom asked. "And isn't it true that they think those questions aren't important ones?"

"Exactly," Jackie confirmed. "And that's why I have to find out just a little bit more about what's going on. Maybe Cosmo is right about Rosie Canty. Her death probably was an accident—even I have to admit that's the most likely explanation now that I've thought about it, but I'm still not completely sure. And there are other things going on downtown that aren't right, and no one seems to be paying any attention."

"What sorts of things are you talking about?" he asked.

Jackie told Tom about the conversation she had overheard between Felix Cockrill and someone named Ivan Hahn, who just might be the same Ivan Hahn who was known to the police as a small-time criminal and strong-arm man in Palmer. She told him about what had happened to George Venable and Eugene Seybold on Saturday night, and why she thought those two things might be connected.

"George and Eugene weren't the first to be targeted," she told him. "This has been going on for weeks, and it's getting worse. Eugene was sent to the hospital. What next? Will someone be killed? Has someone already been killed?"

"Don't you think Evan's got all that under control?" Tom asked her, concern still troubling his eyes as he looked at her.

"Evan's following a different trail right now," said Jackie. "I want to follow this one a little longer, that's all. If I find out they're right, I'll back off and apologize to Evan and Cosmo. And to you." She reached out her hand and put it on his. The contact felt extremely comforting, like always.

"And if you decide you're right?"

"Then I promise I'll take them any evidence I find and let them run with it. I'm not going to go putting myself in the way of guys who put ex-boxers in the hospital."

Tom withdrew his hand, slowly. "I hope that's true," he said. "I hope you won't put yourself in danger." He didn't sound convinced.

Jackie watched as Tom finished making his sandwich, carefully assembling the pieces and cutting it into neat halves, then letting it sit on the plate while he stared at it without seeing.

"I know this bothers you a lot," she said. "I know you'd be a lot happier if I had told you I wasn't the least bit interested in any of this, or if I promised you now that I wasn't going to look any further for those answers I don't know yet."

Tom nodded. "You're right about that."

"But I'd be lying."

"I guess I wouldn't want you to do that," he said carefully.

"But if I did, at least you wouldn't worry so much in

the short term," Jackie supplied, trying to guess at his thoughts.

"Yes, it would make the short term a lot easier to handle," Tom agreed. "But I'm not in this for the short term, Jackie."

"I know."

"And I'm not about to ask you to stop looking for the truth, when it's that passion for justice that's one of the things I love most about you." He touched her face gently with his fingers. "But it's that same need you have to make everything right for everybody that puts you in danger sometimes." He paused and took a shaky breath before going on. "And that frightens the hell out of me, because I honestly don't know what I'd do if I lost you."

Tears stung Jackie's eyes. Her throat ached, and she swallowed hard as she pulled Tom's hand closer. "I'm not going to do anything stupid," she said finally, and hoped fervently that she was telling the absolute truth.

"No, of course you're not," Tom told her. He even looked like he believed it. "Let's eat lunch and take Jake for a walk."

Jake perked up his ears at the sound of his name and the word "walk," one of his favorites. He trotted over to the door as if waiting for Jackie and Tom to stop eating and get to the important stuff.

The temperature was on its way to downright warm as Jackie, Tom, and Jake strolled around the grounds of the kennel. Tom ran Jake over a series of low hurdles that had been set up for obedience training on the weekend. Jake took them easily, and acted eager to go back and do it again. "Okay, Jake," Tom told him, "if you're feeling young enough to do it again, so am I. I'm not the one who has to jump."

Jackie leaned against an oak tree and watched them. They got on very well together. For that matter, Tom and Peter got on very well together, too, and she was crazy about Tom's daughter, Grania. Even Frances approved of Tom, and that couldn't be said for all of the other choices

Jackie had made where men were concerned. And Tom was genuinely fond of Frances. Did this mean they had what it took to become a real family? Or was it she who didn't have what it took? Jackie wished she knew the answer to that one.

Jake finished his second go at the hurdles, and this time he didn't run back to the beginning, but walked over to Jackie and sat down by her, tongue lolling out happily. "I think twice was plenty for him," said Tom, joining them. "Let's go up on the hill over there and sit under the big tree for a while. There aren't going to be many more of these warm, sunny days this year."

"Not much like California, is it?" Jackie teased, putting her arm around him and drawing him closer as they walked up the hill overlooking the kennel buildings.

"True, but then California didn't have you," said Tom. "You're worth any amount of snow and ice and freezing nights, especially if I can cuddle up to you while it's freezing."

The closer they got to the top of the hill and the big tree, the more eager Jake seemed to grow, pulling on his lead until he almost had Jackie off her feet. "Whoa, Jake!" she cautioned.

"I wonder what's got into him?" Tom remarked.

"Maybe just the squirrels," said Jackie. "I saw a lot of them around earlier."

Tom looked thoughtful. "If I know Jake, he doesn't usually get this excited about something as ordinary as a squirrel." He held out his hand and Jackie passed him the end of the lead.

Jake pulled Tom up to the top of the rise and started circling the tree excitedly. He sniffed at something on the ground, then barked and backed off, waiting for Tom to pay attention to his find.

"What is it?" Jackie asked, running to catch up. "What did Jake find?"

"Something truly hideous," said Tom, who had knelt down to get a closer look. He pointed at the ground in front of him as Jackie came up behind him and laid a hand on his shoulder for support.

It was hideous, all right. There on the grass under the oak tree was Alice Roosevelt's missing white enamel poodle earring.

CHAPTER 22

"I don't know about you, but I'd say that's evidence of a sort, wouldn't you, Evan?" Bernie Youngquist examined the earring through the clear plastic of the sandwich bag Jackie had carefully scooped it into from the ground under the oak tree at Cusack Kennels. "You say the woman's name is Alice Roosevelt?"

"That's not her real name, but it's what she calls herself. She has this notion that her father is the President—Theodore Roosevelt. The people downtown who know her call her that, too."

"Yeah, and I'll bet they call her a few other things besides," Evan commented, twirling his index finger beside his ear.

"She's definitely not what you'd call stable," Jackie confirmed. "I'm no psychiatrist, mind you, but in my experience sane people don't go around trying to set other people on fire."

"I'd call that a definite behavior problem," Bernie said, nodding. "Who'd she try to set on fire?"

"Me, for one," said Jackie. "When I tried to ask her questions about Rosie Canty."

"You keep stirring up crap about that Canty woman and *I'll* set you on fire," Evan grumbled.

"You were the one who told me the case was closed," Jackie told him. "Right here in your office—only yesterday, as I recall.'' She didn't mention that she'd been asking questions around town for some time before that.

''That doesn't mean it doesn't make the hairs stand up on the back of my neck when I find out you're out there playing cop again.'' Evan held up the sandwich bag. ''This is—*possibly*—evidence that some jewelry-collecting nutball was out at your boyfriend's place of business. I doubt seriously the evidence techs are going to get any kind of prints off of it, but if Alice Nutcase still has the matching one, you could make a case for her having dropped it there.''

''Yeah, you've got to admit there aren't that many of those classy little items running around loose in central Ohio,'' said Bernie, pointing a cautious finger at the white poodle. ''At least I hope there aren't.'' She shuddered.

''I know what you mean,'' Jackie told her. ''I'm afraid I might have poodle nightmares when I close my eyes tonight.''

''Savage, red-eyed poodle nightmares,'' Bernie agreed solemnly.

''What it *isn't* evidence of,'' Evan continued as though he hadn't heard them, ''is that Alice Wacko tried to torch your boyfriend's kennel. All by itself it isn't proof of much except circumstantially, and what it definitely isn't proof of,'' here he paused to frown at them both, ''is that either Alice Nutso or what happened at Cusack Kennels has anything at all to do with mysterious mustachioed men beating up homeless guys.''

Evan was warming up now, and Jackie and Bernie watched in rapt fascination as he waved the bagged earring around. ''And it's absolutely, positively, *not* proof,'' he finished, ''that any of this is related to some poor drunk dying of exposure in an alley last Wednesday night.''

''I'd like to hear what else Jackie may have heard or seen when she met Alice Roosevelt,'' said Bernie. ''After all, she's actually talked to her—it could be helpful to us.''

Evan gave her a whose-side-are-you-on-anyway kind of look, but what he said was, ''Okay. Sure. Why not?'' He waved a hand at Bernie as if to give her permission to proceed with what he was pretty sure was a harebrained idea.

"Go ahead, Jackie," Bernie said. "Tell us all about Alice."

Jackie related everything she could remember about Alice's appearance and manner, the contents of her beloved pillowcase, and the acrid smell of fuel that clung about her.

"Whoever tried to burn down Cusack Kennels used some kind of hot-burning fuel," Bernie reminded Evan. Evan nodded and made a note of it in a spiral notebook.

"And she did have that box of matches," Jackie recalled. "The ones she lit and threw at me. Laura took them away from her after that."

"Well, it wouldn't be hard to get hold of more if she wanted them," said Bernie. "It's possible she's a pyromaniac, I guess."

"Or maybe she just needs to light fires to stay warm this time of year," Evan put in. "The patrols down in that neighborhood are always having to put out little cookfires and campfires that might spread to nearby buildings. You feel sorry for someone who needs to stay warm, but you can't go around letting them burn down the city, either."

"She was angry at Rosie," Jackie noted. "Laura said they fought from time to time. She also said Alice could get physically violent, though she didn't think she had ever hurt Rosie."

"I'm not even going down that path," said Evan. "Nobody murdered that woman."

"But you'll at least investigate Alice Roosevelt?" Jackie asked. "This evidence does link her to Cusack Kennels."

"You say she spends a lot of time at the Downtown Women's Shelter?"

"That's right. She doesn't live there, but she visits from time to time. Laura's been encouraging her to come by and stay the night ever since what happened to Rosie."

"Well, that's where we'll start looking for her, then," said Evan. "Thanks for this," he said, holding up the poodle in the bag. "Who knows—it may turn out to be something, and it's something we probably wouldn't have without you and Jake.'' He ignored Bernie's look of frank surprise.

Jackie fought the urge to stare, open-mouthed, at Evan Stillman. Two heartfelt compliments in two days, and this one in front of an unimpeachable witness. Her luck might be on the upswing, after all.

''I still say my cousin the gangster beats your great-great-grandfather the fugitive,'' said Grania Cusack, green eyes twinkling. The kids were sitting in the hall outside Peter's room, legs stuck through the wrought-iron railing and dangling over the lower floor where their parents were collaborating on an Italian dinner. ''If you want to top that,'' Grania told Peter, ''you'll have to come up with something a lot more exciting.''

''I'll bet I do,'' Peter countered. ''I've only just got started on my dad's side of the family.''

''A week's allowance?'' Grania challenged.

''Hey, no gambling on the relatives!'' Tom yelled up at them. ''I'm sure Peter's ancestors are every bit as reprehensible as ours. Maybe more so.''

Jackie pulled her head out of the refrigerator. ''I've got everything we need for Capellini Pomidoro,'' she told Tom.

''Fresh basil?''

''Fresh yesterday,'' she assured him. ''And it'll be quick.''

''Let's do it, then,'' said Tom.

''Okay,'' Jackie said, ''I'll get the water going.'' She pulled the spaghetti pot out of a lower cupboard and ran water into it.

''I hope I'm not going to be sorry I asked,'' Tom said, ''but what did Evan and Bernie say about the poodle earring?''

''They were cautiously optimistic about it meaning something,'' said Jackie. ''I think they're planning to talk to Alice Roosevelt soon.''

Jackie had explained the significance of the horrible earring, and told Tom about her encounter with Alice on Sunday. It hadn't done a lot for his fears that she was getting in over her head. At least he'd been given some hope that the person who'd tried to burn down the kennels would be taken into custody.

"I'm having a hard time figuring out why a woman I've never met set fire to my business," he told Jackie, not for the first time that day.

"The way I figure it, she was after Arlo," Jackie explained to him. "She was carrying around a newspaper article about him being rescued from the alley, and it mentioned you, too, for which we can thank Marcella and her love of the human-interest angle. If Alice killed Rosie, she might have decided to finish off her dog, too. No witnesses." She handed Tom a plastic bag of fresh tomatoes and a knife.

"I'm not sure how much of a witness Arlo would make," Tom observed as he started to chop the tomatoes.

"What makes you think he wouldn't be a perfectly fine witness?" Jackie asked him.

"He might do okay at first," Tom admitted with a grin, "but I have a feeling the defense could tear him apart in cross-examination."

"Okay, so he can't talk. But I shouldn't have to remind you that dogs are intelligent in ways humans aren't. If it were Jake who knew what the perpetrator smelled like, he'd identify them for us, and I'll bet Arlo could too. That's why Alice had to get rid of him. Only she bungled the job."

"Well, I'm thankful for that, at least," said Tom. "Where's that basil? And the garlic. We need lots of garlic. You can't have too much fresh garlic in Capellini Pomidoro."

"Hmmm. I think maybe I'd better kiss you *now*," said Jackie.

And she did.

CHAPTER 23

When Rodgers University had been built, back in the late nineteenth century when the Farmers' & Growers' Market was still years in the future, it had been on the outskirts of Palmer, with acres of undeveloped land on all sides.

Nowadays those acres were filled with buildings and lawns and walkways and students (more of those every year) and staff (not nearly enough of those for the past several years). The former outskirts, once farmlands, were now well within the expanded city limits, less than a mile from Jackie's downtown condo.

On nice days she liked to walk to the campus and back, especially since she'd been making an effort to get more exercise, but this being the midwest that wasn't possible for much of the year, and not desirable for a lot of the rest of it. This morning there had been a layer of frost on the ground and a decided nip in the air when it was time to leave for the campus, so Jackie had given in to convenience and driven to work.

Her Tuesday morning Film and Society class went by quickly in a spirited discussion of post-war American culture and 1950s' sensibilities as portrayed by the Great American Movie Machine of Hollywood. Jackie had found herself, given the recent drift of her thoughts, dwelling on how absent the problem of homelessness seemed to be from that Postwar era as she had seen it portrayed in films.

Could it really have been so? Aside from a few hope-lessly alcoholic men sleeping in big-city doorways, were there really no homeless people to speak of in those days? Or were they there and simply overlooked by Hollywood?

Once the nation recovered from the Great Depression, Jackie remembered her parents telling her, it was no longer common to see men selling apples on the street, or families with nowhere to live, like the thousands that had left the dust bowl for the promise of California.

There were always people with no resources, even after the economic recovery of the forties, but they were called bums, and didn't have a lot in common with the suddenly homeless of the eighties. Hardly anyone seemed to stop and think of what a bum might have been a short time before, or whether he might be something different in the future.

It would be another generation before the creation of an entirely new underclass of people forced out of jobs and houses and hope. In that time, which Jackie remembered quite clearly, people who had been able to get by and even own houses found themselves homeless overnight—so many of them that existing agencies were powerless to help more than a tiny percentage without gearing up for the mas-sive numbers of them that seemed to appear out of nowhere in the eighties, thrown on the mercy of trickle-down eco-nomics.

"Ms. Walsh?"

"I'm sorry, John. I was on another planet there for a minute."

"That's okay," said John McBride. "I spent most of my high school years in outer space. Maybe we're neighbors."

The other students snickered appreciatively. John Mc-Bride was one of those students that make teachers remem-ber what drew them to the profession in the first place. In addition to a gratifyingly quick mind, he had an intuitive knack for visual storytelling that gladdened the heart of the entire faculty of the Film Department, and Jackie had a bet going with herself that he'd be a hot young independent filmmaker some day.

"Did you have a question for me, John?" Jackie asked him.

"I guess I was just wondering about some of the differences between Post World War Two America and Post Vietnam America," said John. "There seemed to be a unity of purpose back here on the home front during World War Two that was entirely lacking twenty years later. Do you think that was just Hollywood hype, or were things really different then?"

"Well, I don't think war itself was a lot different as far as the day-to-day experiences of the people fighting it," said Jackie, "but our notions of what war was, and what actually went on in one, were certainly a lot more naive."

"Yeah, we were the 'good guys' in that war," said someone at the back of the room.

"Exactly," Jackie agreed. "And that, and a certain amount of naiveté on the home front, had a completely different effect on the military personnel returning home. The hell they'd been through was a lot like the one their children and grandchildren would go through in Vietnam twenty-some years later, but they were coming home to a society that was considerably less psychologically sophisticated."

"So they had the same problems, but fewer mechanisms for dealing with it. Is that what you mean?" John McBride asked.

"Yes," Jackie said, "but there were advantages for them, too, over the Vietnam veterans. Remember, the folks at home were pretty well united in their belief in the rightness of the war and the heroism of the military. That was definitely not going to be the case twenty years down the road."

"It probably didn't help that in the sixties we had the war coming right into our living rooms," remarked Marti Bernstein. Marti, Palmer's last hippie, was also Rodgers University's oldest student, and no doubt remembered the daily dose of Vietnam everyone received at home, instead of having to read about it in history books like the rest of the class.

"Right," said Jackie. "During the Second World War people had to rely on newspapers, radio, and newsreels. None of those are as intensely personal as television, because none of them live in your home like a member of your family. It gave those people a whole different take on the subject of war.

"Society itself was also radically different," Jackie went on. "The idea that just because someone was in authority didn't automatically make them right was gaining popular currency. Some people became conscious of the fact that this war wasn't like the ones their fathers and grandfathers had gone off to, and they weren't shy about saying it."

She checked her watch. Class was almost over. "Well, we're veering off the subject slightly, but I just wanted to say it's been a good class today—nearly all of us stayed awake."

The bell rang, and the end-of-class shuffle commenced up in the rows of seats. "We'll cover Post-Vietnam films later in the semester, of course," she called to the departing students. "See you Thursday."

Someone was in the open doorway, breasting the tide of students, creating little eddies of humanity as they flowed around her and out onto the walkway outside the classroom. Jackie looked closer at the figure silhouetted against the bright sunlight outside. It was Emma Cockrill.

Jackie had almost forgotten that before she left Emma alone and unsupported in the echoing expanses of the Cockrill mansion on Sunday afternoon, she had given in to a sympathetic impulse and invited her to join her for lunch today. It seemed the least she could do to return the dubious favor of an invitation to Felix and Ada Cockrill's impressive fifteen-room bungalow, though Emma would have to make do with a restaurant meal today.

"Hi there," Jackie greeted her. "You're a little early for lunch, I'm afraid."

"Oh, I gave Eden a ride to her ten o'clock class and I was just walking around the campus," said Emma, stepping inside the room. "I can come back again closer to lunchtime."

She looked around the classroom. "This puts me in mind of my own college days," she said. "Though I never studied film, of course. After Ella . . ." She paused, unable to say the word. "After that I went back to school, but it was never quite the same without her to liven things up. The next three years were entirely too peaceful, I'm afraid."

"Why don't you walk with me over to my office," Jackie offered, "and I'll put this stuff away." She motioned to a pile of books and papers that littered the surface of the desk. "I have to be back on campus at two o'clock, and I need to go home for something before lunch, so you can ride along with me, if you have that much time to kill."

"I have nothing but time to kill," said Emma. "I'd love to go along with you."

"Welcome to my humble abode," said Jackie, unlocking the front door to her apartment and standing aside so that Emma could enter before her.

Emma stepped inside, gazing up and around at the high ceilings and the red brick walls with their tall, narrow windows. "Your home is so unusual!" she exclaimed. "And so creative!"

"It used to be half of an industrial building," Jackie explained. "They split it down the middle and sold it as two condos when they revamped the neighborhood a few years ago."

"Oh, and look at all the wonderful artwork!" She craned her neck to take in the large, colorful posters Jackie had hung everywhere on the walls, clear up to the high ceilings where pipes and ducts crisscrossed the room, industrial-style.

"It's just a lot of old movie posters," said Jackie. "I guess some of them are probably valuable to a collector, but that's not why I have them. I can't imagine ever parting with them for money." She set her handbag down on the dining table and looked around for Jake and Charlie.

"Jake! Charlie!" she called. "Anyone for a romp in the yard before I have to leave again? Last chance, guys!"

"Who are Jake and Charlie?" Emma inquired, looking around her.

Jake trotted out of Peter's room at the top of the stairs with a fuzzy ginger streak zipping past his feet and bouncing down the stairway ahead of him. The big Shepherd negotiated the circular iron stairs with a bit more dignity than his feline pal, descending at a pace that better suited his maturity.

"Jake's my dog," Jackie began, as the Shepherd stopped at the bottom of the stairs and growled low in his throat. Jackie turned at the sound and saw that his head was lowered as he looked at Emma from between his front legs, and the hair on his neck was standing up like a canine mohawk.

Charlie seemed to catch Jake's sense of alarm and struck a Halloween cat pose with his four feet planted close together and his back arched, short orange fur standing out from his spine like little spikes. Then he screeched like a banshee and took off in a dead run for the safety of the kitchen.

Jackie turned back and looked at Emma, who was staring wide-eyed at Jake.

"He won't hurt you. I don't think," she added, almost to herself. She had never seen Jake react quite like this to an unexpected houseguest. "Jake, calm down! I really don't know what's the matter with him. I'm terribly sorry."

Emma's mouth worked for a moment without any intelligible sounds emerging. "I'm quite frightened of dogs," she managed finally in a hoarse whisper. "I always have been. They can sense it, I'm afraid—they all seem to have this reaction."

She stood completely still, her unbandaged arm clutching the bandaged one. She seemed afraid to move for fear of being attacked. The way Jake was acting right now, Jackie could certainly understand her caution.

"I'm really sorry—I'll just put him outside," said Jackie. She gripped Jake's collar firmly in one hand and pulled him toward the kitchen.

"You're going outside before you frighten my guest to

death,'' she muttered at him. Charlie was already at the back door, a bit calmer now, and Jackie let them both outside. ''I'll be back after lunch to let you back in,'' she told Jake with a disapproving frown. ''See if you can get a grip between now and then.''

CHAPTER 24

Jackie returned to the front room, where Emma was sitting on a chair and fanning herself shakily with this month's copy of *Movie Maker*. "Are you all right?" Jackie asked her. "Can I get you something to drink? A glass of water?"

"I'm fine, really," Emma insisted, sounding considerably less than fine. "You mustn't worry about me. I think there's just something about me that makes animals nervous."

Jackie could certainly understand that—there were plenty of things about Emma that made *her* nervous, too, mainly the fact that she never seemed in the least relaxed herself.

"I thought we might eat downtown," said Jackie. "How about Suzette's?"

"Certainly," said Emma. "I'm sure that will be just fine."

Hindsight being a perfect twenty-twenty, Jackie wondered after they sat down if Suzette's had been such a good choice, and if she'd have made another if she had been thinking straight. She knew that both Cosmo and Marcella had been known to come here at lunchtime, and she didn't really want to run into anyone she knew this afternoon.

The purpose of this lunch, after all, was to get Emma Cockrill to come out of her shell a bit, and possibly even enjoy herself. After the fright Jake had given her, Jackie was afraid that goal had been set back just a bit. Emma had seemed more than usually withdrawn as she sat in the passenger seat of Jackie's Blazer on the way to the restaurant and watched downtown Palmer go by outside the car windows.

"Is there someplace you'd rather eat than Suzette's?" she had asked Emma, who had been staring out the window with unfocused eyes. "It's a crêperie, and I didn't even think to ask if you like crêpes."

"I'm afraid I don't go out much," Emma apologized. "I usually just eat at home with Mother."

When Emma said that, Jackie knew for certain that she was doing the right thing sparing her another joyless luncheon experience with Ada Cockrill. She felt like a regular Girl Scout performing a chancy but worthwhile rescue. "Well, I think you'll like this place," she told her. "It's very homey and comfortable, and the crêpes are heavenly."

"I'm sure it will be fine," said Emma. "I do love crêpes," she added.

Emma did seem genuinely pleased with Suzettes' ambience, and delighted with the menu. After a bit of consideration she ordered the Leek and Goat Cheese crêpe and a pot of Earl Grey tea.

Jackie couldn't resist the lure of the wild mushrooms and ordered that one again with great anticipation, and in keeping with a spirit of adventure, a cup of Suzettes' killer coffee. She congratulated herself all the while on doing a good deed for poor Emma.

Jackie felt guilty to be thinking of Emma Cockrill as "poor Emma," but the mousy little woman seemed to invite that sort of adjective. It didn't help that she seemed almost pitifully happy to be out socializing once she'd gotten over her earlier upset. She stared around at Suzettes' walls and floor and furnishings, seeming to compare them favorably to the sort of opulence she lived with every day of her life. "I love this place," she told Jackie. "I'm so glad I accepted your invitation to lunch. I almost didn't, you know."

"Well, I understand you might have been busy," said Jackie. She didn't really think Emma had been busy, but she felt like she ought to give her some way of keeping face.

"I'm never busy," said Emma frankly. "It's just difficult for me to leave the house. For several years, I didn't leave at all." She tried on a bright smile. "I'm getting much better at it lately, though."

"I'm glad to hear it," said Jackie. "There's a lot more to life than sitting around the house, no matter how lovely a house it may be."

"I'm beginning to find that out," said Emma. Their crêpes arrived, and she tasted hers with real delight. "Oh, my, this is good."

"And you're used to good," Jackie observed, "so coming from you that's a rave review for this place."

"I'm so glad we came," Emma said, with real emotion. "I can't say I've ever truly been happy since . . . what happened to my sister twenty years ago, but I'm learning to enjoy life a bit more, and to take action instead of always waiting to be acted upon. I'm beginning to learn what I'm capable of," she said, cutting another bit of crêpe. "Perhaps I will be happy again, someday."

"I'm glad you told me about Ella," said Jackie. "I know how important she must have been to you, and I get the feeling you don't have the chance to talk about her too often."

"No, I don't," said Emma quietly. "And there's more to the story—so much more. I think you're the only person I can trust with the rest of it."

Jackie held up a hand. "Please don't feel like you have to tell me anything you'd rather not," she said, remembering Frances' Saturday morning speculations on Emma's past. "I'll understand if you choose not to."

"Oh, no," Emma told her. "I really feel like I ought to. I want to."

"Ella started sneaking out to see Mr. Burke soon after we started his English class in the autumn of our first year," Emma said to Jackie. The server had cleared away their lunch dishes and brought around a second cup of coffee.

"I warned her she'd be expelled if anyone ever found out, but she was in love, or so she said."

"And how about him? Do you think Mr. Burke was in love with Ella?"

Jackie and Emma were nearly alone in Suzette's, the lunch crowd and most of the lunchtime employees being long gone, and Jackie having slipped away for a moment to call a colleague in her department and ask him to stick a note to her door explaining she wouldn't be in for her office hours today. Emma Cockrill was in a mood to tell more stories about her family, and Jackie seemed unable to ignore the opportunity to hear them.

She felt almost guilty sitting here listening to these confidences being aired for her, a near stranger. There was something not quite right about it, but somewhere in there might be the key to what had happened to Emma to remove from her all hope of a normal, satisfying life, and Jackie couldn't help wanting to know what that was, and if anything might still be done about it after all these years.

"I'm sure he was only taking advantage of her inexperience," said Emma in reply to Jackie's question. Her voice grew harsh as she spoke the words, and her eyes narrowed. "He was not a good man."

They had worked their way up from childhood, with stories of the usual twin hijinks, such as the sisters switching outfits in the middle of the day at school to confuse their teachers, or both claiming to be Ella if it were Emma who was in trouble. Like any imaginative youngsters they made a regular hobby out of confounding their parents and other adults, and being twins they found more opportunities than most to do so. Even Ada's attempts at pruning them to fit her long-range plans couldn't put an end to all of it.

Now that Emma's account had arrived at the first year the twins had spent away at college, and with the appearance of the handsome Timothy Burke, an English instructor not more than a few years older than Emma and Ella, the plot was beginning to thicken. There had been a strong and immediate attraction between her sister and the young instructor, and it was not in Ella's nature to deny that attraction merely because some silly old rules forbade it.

"When I found out she'd been . . . intimate . . . with him, I threatened to tell Mother. Ella told me she'd kill herself if I did. I believed her." Here she paused for a moment as if uncertain whether she should go on. Then she took a deep breath and went on. "In January, Ella told me she was pregnant."

"And did she tell Mr. Burke, too?" Jackie wanted to know.

"Yes," said Emma. "Soon after that he left town and never came back, as far as I know."

"How awful for her! What did she do then?"

"She stayed in school and swore me to silence. I ate like a pig for the next four months so I'd gain weight as she did, and make her less conspicuous. It seemed to work— she didn't get very large until just before her time, and she had no close friends. Neither of us did, except for one another. Finally, though, the school year was over, and we had to go home."

"And of course your mother knew as soon as she saw her, didn't she?"

"She did," said Emma.

"She would," said Jackie. She couldn't imagine Ada Cockrill's hard little green eyes missing much of what went on around her.

"She took us both away immediately to a small town in upstate New York, where she rented a house and arranged for Ella to give birth in a private hospital when her time came."

"And then she adopted the baby," said Jackie. Of course. Suddenly her mother's harebrained idea about Ada and Eden made perfect sense. Frances had pegged the wrong Cockrill daughter as Eden's mother, but she hadn't known of Ella's existence.

"That's right," said Emma. "Ella didn't want to give up her child, but she lost a lot of her spirit when Mr. Burke went away. The will to fight Mother seemed to have gone out of her. Eden was born in early August. In September Ella and I went back to school."

"You told me she killed herself during your second year at college," Jackie remembered.

Emma nodded. "It was evident to me that Ella wasn't well. I tried to tell Mother, but she ignored me as usual—said Ella would get better in time, but she never did. That was why Mother was able to browbeat her into signing Eden away to her, of course. She seemed to have no will of her own—so different from the Ella we'd all known before.

"Things just went from bad to worse after school started," Emma continued. "Ella missed classes, and she didn't seem to see or hear anything in the ones she did attend." She paused and swallowed, going on with difficulty. "As the year went on she became completely despondent. Just before Christmas vacation she jumped off a tall bridge near the campus and drowned."

Emma's voice faded to nearly nothing as she finished her story, and Jackie found herself leaning forward to catch the last few words: "The body was never found." Then silence, broken only by the sound of Emma's ragged breathing.

"Oh here you are!" Marcella's voice plucked Jackie's nerves like an overstretched guitar string. She jumped several inches, and Emma Cockrill jumped in the opposite direction as Marcella bore down on them, newspaper in hand.

"Please tell me it was you who discovered the body," Marcella pleaded, pulling up a chair and sitting down opposite Jackie. "Restore my faith in the weirdness of fate."

Jackie waited for her heart rate to approach normal before responding to Marcella. Finally she said, "If there were any bodies discovered in this town since last Thursday morning, they were found by somebody else. Honest." She crossed her heart to emphasize her innocence and complete uninvolvement and took a bracing swallow of her coffee. Then it occurred to her to wonder. "Uh, exactly what body are we talking about, anyway?"

Marcella handed her the paper, unfolded to the story in the Local News section. "Another homeless woman. This one had a name—a long Polish one, as I remember. But being just a bit deluded,'' Marcella made a circling motion near her ear, ''she apparently referred to herself as Alice Roosevelt.''

CHAPTER 25

Jackie stared at the newspaper for several seconds, unable to read the words, then at Marcella for several more. "Are you absolutely sure?" she asked Marcella finally.

Marcella pointed at the article. "It's all right there," she said. "I know it's hard to believe—I mean, Alice Roosevelt? Give me a break!"

"I talked to her just the other day," Jackie told her, shaking her head in disbelief.

"You knew this woman?" Marcella gasped.

"You knew her?" Emma echoed.

"I didn't know her well, but Laura Santillo introduced us. I needed to ask her about . . . Oh, it's not important what," Jackie said, realizing that she really didn't want to get into a discussion of her curiosity about Rose Canty with either Emma or Marcella. "But the point is I talked to her only two days ago and now she's dead."

"I hope you're not blaming yourself for this woman's death," said Emma. "That kind of person is bound to meet an unpleasant end, I think. Why, just look at the way they live!"

"Well, I don't see how those two things could be connected anyhow," said Marcella. "So you couldn't possibly blame yourself. I know you have a knack for getting into the middle of this sort of thing, but you don't actually *cause* murders. Do you?" Her eyes widened just a bit.

"That's not what I meant," Jackie told them with just a hint of impatience. "It's just that it's such a . . . a strange feeling."

Strange didn't exactly cover what she was experiencing right now, Jackie realized. She tried to find the words to convey her meaning to the two women, but the unwelcome sensation that had come to rest in the pit of her stomach when Marcella told her Alice Roosevelt was dead was not one·easily dealt with by words.

"We hear every day about people dying, people being murdered," Jackie began, "people we don't know. Then I find a dead woman I also don't know, but I've been finding out more and more about her until I almost feel I do know her. And her death is supposed to be an accident . . ."

"*Supposed* to be?" Marcella and Emma exclaimed in stereo.

"Okay, very likely is an accident," Jackie amended. "And here we are less than a week later, and another woman who was a friend of hers is also dead. Could that be a coincidence? What are the odds, I wonder?"

"Well, this death was no accident," Marcella told her. "Someone hit this woman over the head with something big and heavy, probably several times. Caved her skull right in."

Jackie knew she had to pull herself together somehow. She had managed to drive Emma back to her car at Rodgers after Marcella had left them to return to the *Gazette*, and to get herself home. She had even managed to call Tom and tell him that the woman who had probably set fire to the kennel was dead, but she wondered how much else she would prove capable of today.

She remembered that she had promised Gillian Zane she would attend tonight's City Council meeting—now only three hours away—and having heard Felix Cockrill's opinions on his influence in the city government, she felt the Save the Market campaign could probably use all the warm bodies it could get at tonight's meeting, whether or not they had any hope of actually saving anything.

Before today's revelation about poor Alice Roosevelt, she had actually been thinking about speaking at the meeting, and to that end had dug through her recycle pile of old newspapers and found all five parts of Marcella's series on Market Place. Thankfully, she wasn't usually too quick to bundle the papers and leave them out for the truck that came by for them on Mondays, so there was usually quite a stack of them just outside the door from the kitchen to the garage. She'd been hoping to pore over them one more time to reacquaint herself with the important details of the issues involved.

Now the Local News sections of the Palmer *Gazette* containing Marcella's series were lying in a neat stack on the dining room table, but Jackie wasn't sure she had the presence of mind to read the articles with any level of intelligence, much less stand up and give a speech tonight. Today's bombshell about the sudden, violent death of Alice Roosevelt, née Rossovich, had pretty nearly robbed her of the capacity for rational thought.

Jackie had once taken one of those pencil-and-paper stress tests, where you choose from a list of life-changing events those that had happened to you in the past twelve months. Then you added up the points: a marital separation was worth sixty-five points, getting fired from your job counted for fifty, a mortgage foreclosure was good for thirty. Even happy events like a marriage or a career accomplishment took their toll. When you added it all up, the higher your numbers were the more likely you were supposed to be to come down with depression or some other illness on account of stress.

Jackie supposed she needed a completely different list for her rather peculiar stress factors: Find Dead Body, seventy-five; Suffer From Unfounded Jealousy, fifty. Get Involved in Hopeless Restoration Campaign, thirty. And how about Investigate Mysterious Goings-On? One hundred and ten, easy. She didn't feel ill yet, and she wasn't depressed exactly, but her system didn't feel ready for another shock right now.

Maybe focusing on the Market Place issue and the importance of preserving Farmers' & Growers' would be a good way to take her mind off dead women in alleyways, she thought. It was worth a try. After collecting a pen and a notepad to help her organize her thoughts, and making herself a cup of jasmine tea, Jackie sat down in front of the papers and picked up the top one.

"Hi, Mom!" The front door banged open and shut again. Peter came into the kitchen with an armful of books. Jackie smiled at her son, who was rapidly turning into a pretty neat young man, despite having the normal afflictions of a teenager. She felt better already, just seeing him home.

"I'm starved," he announced. "Is there anything here to eat?"

Jake, who had been napping under the table with his buddy Charlie between his paws, recognized one of those all-important words he knew so well, and came scooting out, looking around for what was being offered. He shoved his nose into Peter's hand.

"Hiya, Jake," Peter said.

"You know," Jackie told her red-headed teenager, "if I were a gambling woman I could make pretty good money betting that your first words when you come in the door on any day of the week would be some variation on 'what's to eat?' "

"I know what's important in life," said Peter, dumping the books on top of Jackie's papers and opening the refrigerator door.

"Yeah. Cold pizza."

"Have we got any?" Peter asked eagerly, looking through the refrigerator's contents.

"I don't think so, but since your grandma and I have to go out for a while tonight, maybe we can arrange for some of the fresh, hot stuff."

"Gourmet Veggie with Garlic Sauce? And a couple of videos?"

"Anything you want," she promised expansively. Peter was great about being left home alone for a few hours if he could be compensated with a couple of martial arts movies. "How about *Best of the Best 1* and *2*?" she offered, naming two of Peter's favorites.

"How about *The Perfect Weapon* and *Street Knight*?" Peter countered. "Those have a lot of good Kenpo fighting stuff."

"It's a deal," Jackie said. "I'll run out and get the eats and the movies a little later. Now take these books upstairs, okay? I have to read these newspaper articles you buried under them before I go to the City Council meeting tonight."

Peter picked up the books, his quest for a snack temporarily forgotten. "I thought somebody said you can't fight City Hall," he remarked, "whatever the heck that means."

"I think it means little people who don't have a lot of money or influence to throw around don't stand a snowball's chance in Hell against powerful business interests who create jobs for the city and play tennis with the mayor," Jackie ventured. "But somebody's got to try."

"Well, I'm sure you and Grandma'll show 'em how it's done," said Peter, giving her shoulder a companionable slap. He bounded up the iron stairs two at a time and into his room.

Jackie could hear the books hitting the floor upstairs. "Stop abusing your homework!" she called up to him, then turned what attention she could back to the newspapers. She read through the first article, which had appeared last Wednesday, taking a few notes as she went. This one had followed fairly closely on the heels of Felix Cockrill's announcement of his plan to modernize the Market District, and included Jay Garnett's sketch of the finished complex.

Seeing the sketch again reminded her of Jay and Gillian, and she hoped they'd worked something out between them Sunday, or at least begun talking about the problem. When she'd finally opened up to Tom about her irrational jealousy of Bernie Youngquist, he'd been able to quiet her fears in a matter of seconds. Communication was often difficult, she reminded herself, but nearly always beneficial in the long run, once you made yourself get over the pain of actually having to bare your soul to someone.

The second article had appeared in Thursday's paper. That was the one Rosie Canty had been carrying in her pocket when she died. Jackie read this one over with a sense of sadness as she thought how, on the last day of her life, the homeless woman had torn out and saved this page with its dispassionate discussion of issues that were so vital to her future.

Except Rosie Canty hadn't had any future, Jackie thought, but of course she hadn't had any way of knowing that. No one ever knew what tomorrow might bring, and that included safe, secure people with warm beds to sleep in at night. She turned the page.

The next page of the Local News section was devoted to the weather forecast, an article on a new freeway off-ramp which, Jackie felt sure, would probably spawn four more generic coffee shops, a profile of a local chainsaw sculptor, and an article about some Rodgers University students who were interning at businesses around town. Jackie was surprised to see Eden Cockrill in a group photograph of the students. Eden was apparently earning credits toward her biology degree by working part-time at the North Palmer Animal Clinic. "I guess some practical experience ought to give her an idea whether she really wants to be a vet," Jackie said to herself as she put down the second newspaper and picked up the third.

Friday's paper had been the one that carried the article about Rosie Canty's death, but that had been in the front section. Peter, fascinated as any kid his age with that sort of thing, had saved that page even though it didn't actually mention Jackie by name, a fact for which she was terribly grateful.

When she had worked her way clear through Sunday, the paper that had caused all the flap in the Cockrill household, Jackie felt a great deal readier to speak her mind on the subject of the Market District's future and the folly of Felix Cockrill's notion of remaking Palmer in his own image.

She called Guido's and ordered the pizza, but decided against taking Jake along to pick it up. Good manners or no, it was unfair to subject the poor guy to the aroma of parmesan and romano cheeses all the way home in the car. She absorbed his reproachful look as she closed the door. "Sorry, boy. Maybe if you're lucky, Peter will let you have his crusts."

CHAPTER 26

The buzz of a dozen simultaneous conversations in the Palmer City Council chambers at City Hall greeted Jackie and Frances as they arrived at a few minutes before seven-thirty that evening. "There's something I've been trying to remember that I wanted to tell you," said Frances as they walked inside, "but I can't remember for the life of me what it was."

"It'll come back to you, Mother," Jackie assured her. "It always does."

Mayor Bellamy and the council members were nowhere in sight as yet, but Felix and Ada Cockrill were there, chatting up a tight little knot of downtown businessmen who were known or felt to be strongly in favor of Market Place. As nearly as Jackie could tell from the faces she could recognize, the Cockrills' supporters were drawn mainly from the moneyed and usually conservative section of the city. Many of the people who supported Gillian Zane and the Save the Market campaign were drawn from the artistic and academic quarters, though not all, by any means.

Cosmo Gordon was visible on the opposite side of the room from the Cockrills, talking with Blair Brotherton of Brotherton's Department Store, and some of the other people Jackie had seen at the Save the Market meeting on Friday night. Hardly anyone was sitting down yet, but apparently sides had already been drawn before she and

Frances arrived, like iron filings lining up on either end of a magnet, and it was pro Market Place on the right, pro Farmers' and Growers' on the left. The numbers looked pretty even so far.

They headed left for friendly territory, and Frances went off to talk with Marianne Chung, the T.V. chef. She had been hoping to run into her again ever since the Friday night meeting so she could try to wrangle her recipe for Pumpkin and Carrot Soup.

"Hi, Jackie!" Marcella said cheerily. "I hope you're feeling better." Marcella was carrying a little cassette recorder, the better to capture those historic moments, and leading around a rather overwhelmed photographer who was not Leo McTaggart.

"Lots, thanks. That was just a bit of a nasty shock. I hope I didn't freak out on you too badly this afternoon."

"Don't give it another thought," Marcella said.

"Where's Leo?" Jackie inquired.

Marcella pointed to a corner on the left-hand side where Leo and Eden Cockrill were deep in conversation with a handsome gray-haired man Jackie recognized as Morgan Jones, the Senior Editor at Rodgers University Press. "He called this morning to say he wouldn't be available tonight. Seems he's got better things to do, and who could blame him?"

"I notice Cosmo seems to have allied himself with the F and G faction, too," Jackie observed.

"Well, we always knew he would, didn't we?" said Marcella. "I may not agree with Cosmo about this, but I admire him for being willing to make a stand."

"He's an admirable man," Jackie observed.

"You've got that right," Marcella agreed, "but I hope you both know there's not a chance of swaying the council on Market Place—they've got big, shining dollar signs in their eyes."

"It's not over yet," said Jackie.

"I'll be here when it is, one way or the other," said Marcella, "and I'll get to write the story, too. What more could I ask?"

"Sounds like the best of everything to me," said Jackie.

"Come on, Werner, let's go get some graphics," Marcella said to her companion. She gave Jackie a good-bye wave, and the two of them headed off for the power side of the room.

Jackie went to join Leo and Eden and Morgan Jones. "I can't thank you enough for sending me Leo," said Morgan as soon as she came up to them. "He showed me his photos of the Market, and the text he's written to accompany them, and I was quite favorably impressed."

"Mr. Jones has offered Leo a contract," said Eden. "They're going to combine old photos of Farmers' and Growers' from clear back as when it was just a vacant lot, all the way up to Leo's modern shots, and Leo's going to write all the text. Isn't that just wonderful?" She looked at Leo as though she was pretty sure he was what was wonderful, and he blushed becomingly and returned the look with an adoring one of his own.

"So, Morgan," Jackie wanted to know, "are you doing this in anticipation of the Market being saved, or demolished?"

"Well, personally," said Morgan Jones, "I hope we get to keep F and G, but from a publishing standpoint, I can't lose either way."

Gillian Zane arrived, breathless and more than a bit nervous. She spotted Jackie and the others and started making her way toward them, but kept getting stopped by people wanting to make conversation or just wish her well on her attempt to save Farmers' and Growers'.

Jay Garnett came in not long after, and Felix Cockrill spotted him almost immediately and waved him over. Jackie noted with interest that although Jay gave Felix a friendly wave of the hand, he did not join his brother-in-law and sister in the growing group of Palmer citizens who were here to support the shopping complex he had designed for Cockrill Industries. Now *that* was a fascinating turn of events.

The conversation between Leo and Morgan and Eden went on without her while Jackie watched to see what would happen next. Felix said something to Ada, who turned around and looked at her younger brother with a slight frown.

Jay smiled pleasantly at his sister and kept walking in the same direction he'd started until he caught up with Gillian, who had been accosted by a group of enthusiastic pro-F & G people determined to carry on a spirited conversation with her about her proposal for the Market Historic District. She slipped an arm through his and smiled up at him.

Someone in Felix's crowd was tapping him on the shoulder and pointing out a man in dark clothes who was standing just inside the door to the council chambers. The man was looking at Felix, but making no move to come inside. Felix lowered his brows in a deep frown, but walked slowly and carefully to the door. Jackie tried to watch without being unbearably obvious as Felix and the man talked in hushed tones.

Jackie would have given a lot to know what they were talking about, especially since the man was smiling, and even Felix looked pleased, for him. The other reason she would have liked to be a fly on a nearby wall was that the man was tall and thin and had a mustache. After a brief conversation the man turned and left, and Felix returned to his group.

Frances was back with the soup recipe scribbled into her notebook and a self-satisfied smile on her face. "Marianne invited me to a taping of the show next week," she told Jackie. "Isn't that wonderful?"

"There's a whole lot of wonderful going around tonight," Jackie told her with a sigh. "I wish I could get some of it for myself, but if I must, I'll settle for everyone else getting a share."

Cosmo had broken off from the group he'd been talking to earlier and was walking toward them. Jackie turned to meet him. "I'd like to apologize for being such a pain in the butt lately," she said by way of greeting.

"You've never been exactly that," Cosmo told her gently, a slight smile playing around the edges of his mouth.

"You'd say that," she said, "but I know what I'm like

when I get an idea and won't let it go. I haven't given you or Evan a moment's peace about this whole Rosie Canty thing.''

''I understand why you were so interested in the case, Jackie. You don't have to apologize to me. I half expected you to start up all over again when that other woman turned up dead this morning.''

''I know you did, and I'm really sorry. I just somehow feel like, because I found the body and I've met so many people who knew her, that I have some kind of connection with her,'' Jackie tried to explain. ''And I wish there were something I could do to give her another chance. Fifty is too young to freeze to death in a trash can, whether it was an accident or not.''

''You're absolutely right,'' Cosmo agreed. ''What's worse is, she wasn't even nearly fifty years old, by my estimation.''

''But I thought . . .''

''That's what Detective Youngquist estimated on her initial report, yes, but when we got her cleaned up it was obvious Rose Canty was hardly any older than you. Forty, tops, I'd say.''

''Oh!'' said Frances. ''That's what I was trying to remember to tell you on the way over here! I remembered where I'd heard that name before.''

Jackie gave her mother a blank look.

''Canty. Remember? I said I thought I knew somebody by that name, but I never did. It's from Mark Twain. We read a lot of Mark Twain in my book group this summer. It's from *The Prince and the Pauper*. That was the name of the little pauper boy who looked just like the prince. Tom Canty.''

Jackie put a hand on Cosmo's shoulder to steady herself. ''Are you all right?'' he asked her.

''I'm not sure,'' was all she could say for a moment, while her mind raced around in circles. ''Can you give my mother a ride back to my place?''

''Sure, Jackie, but . . .''

''Jacqueline? What's wrong?''

"Nothing's wrong, Mother, I just remembered something, is all." It wasn't so much remembering as frantically trying to piece together fragments of what she already knew, but the conclusion she was coming to was not one she really wanted to deal with. She wondered what the stress charts would make of this one.

A door in the back of the room opened up, and the Mayor and the members of the City Council began to file inside and take their seats at a long table atop a raised dais. People started to take their seats on the right- and left-hand sides of the room.

"Mother, do you think you could make my apologies to Gillian and the others? I was going to give a talk during the public forum part of the meeting, but I'm not going to be able to. There's something I have to do. Could you keep Peter company until I get home? He's got a couple of Jeff Speakman videos," she added as incentive. Frances was mad about Jeff Speakman's muscles.

"For that I'll give your speech for you and pick up popcorn on the way over," Frances promised. "I was planning on standing up and saying a little something anyway," she added modestly.

Jackie knew she was going to be sorry to miss that. "I'm sorry I can't explain right now, but I promise I'll see you later tonight." She thanked Cosmo again, kissed her mother's cheek and hurried outside.

The cool night air cleared her head a little, and Jackie formulated her plan as she walked to her car. She had known all along that the only way to figure out what was really happening in the Market District would be to go out on the streets and find out, but the only practical way to do that would be to become invisible, and she hadn't figured out how to do that until tonight.

The only way to make sure no one will see you while you're out there in plain sight is to become one of the invisible people, Jackie thought as she unlocked her car, started the engine and drove away from Palmer's City Hall complex. The only visible difference between her and a homeless woman was her outward appearance, and that could be changed.

She was only now beginning to realize how completely a person could disappear from the comfortable world she'd always inhabited into the bleak and hungry world of the back streets and alleyways that she had become all too familiar with since Thursday morning. She was only beginning to piece together the seemingly unrelated bits of information she'd acquired over the last five days into a disturbing picture of deception and obsession.

And as much as she hated the thought, she knew she'd have to be the one to tell Emma Cockrill that poor, crazy, dead Rosie Canty was her missing twin, Ella.

CHAPTER 27

South Iowa Street between Fourth and Fifth avenues was dark and quiet this time of the evening. The local businesses, mostly warehouses, parts shops, and wholesale dealers, were locked up and deserted. There were still lights burning in the windows of the Downtown Women's Shelter, and Jackie thought they looked particularly warm and comforting, especially since she had no choice but to remain here outside.

The temperature had dropped sharply since she left the City Council chambers an hour before, with a brisk October wind from the northwest blowing in some more of that icy arctic air, along with a thunderstorm from Ontario that was expected to arrive in force some time tonight. Jackie looked up at the gathering clouds and pulled Peter's jacket closer around her, but it did little to keep the chill out.

Peter had been so engrossed in watching Jeff Speakman's Kenpo moves that he had hardly noticed when Jackie had come home early from the City Council meeting. "So it was that dull, huh?" was his only remark from his favorite T.V.-watching spot on the faux-oriental rug in the living room.

"I had to bug out," said Jackie. "Grandma's coming by in a while to watch movies with you. She's bringing popcorn."

"Cool," said Peter.

She had gone up the stairs to the hallway that led to the two loft bedrooms above the first floor, but after checking to make sure Peter's attention was completely on the television, she had entered his room instead of her own. Closing the door as quietly as she could, she turned on the lamp over his desk and aimed the light low to minimize its visibility from downstairs. With a deep breath, she opened the closet door.

Peter Walsh's closet was the stuff of legend. Darker than the Heart of Africa, more impassable than the Himalayas, more terrifying than Freddy Krueger's nightmares, it could be conquered only by a hero with unlimited courage and unlimited plastic garbage bags. Thankfully, Jackie wasn't here to conquer it, but to take a few things and run. Even so, it was a daunting prospect, and she approached it with almost as much trepidation as the rest of the evening she had mapped out for herself.

A pair of oversized men's pants, an old flannel shirt and a torn windbreaker later, Jackie withdrew from the hazardous realm of the closet and reached for the desk lamp to turn it out. Catching sight of herself in the mirror over Peter's dresser, she realized she'd have to do something about her hair. A knit cap with a Chicago Bulls emblem was thrown over the knob on the back of the desk chair and she decided it would do nicely, turned inside out. She snatched it up, doused the light, and went back downstairs to change in the garage.

Now she wandered up and down the streets of the Market District, seeing few people and fewer cars in the dim glow from the occasional streetlight that wasn't broken or burned out. It could be argued, she supposed, that she should never have come down here, especially at night. This probably wasn't the safest place in town for a woman walking around with no real place to go, but then most women in this situation didn't have an eighty-pound German Shepherd walking around with them.

"When we're home safe and sound tonight, Jake," she told her dog, "remind me why this seemed like such a good idea, okay?"

Jake had nothing to say to that.

Jackie had been painfully aware, on her visits to this part of the neighborhood over the past few days, how much she stood out in her middle-class clothes and her obvious relative prosperity. It had been impossible for her to go unnoticed here, although the homeless people who scraped out a living on these streets by panhandling, distributing flyers, and doing odd jobs for the locals went almost completely unnoticed by everyone around them. The homeless are invisible because we refuse to look at them, Jackie had come to realize.

She wouldn't have the slightest problem describing or recognizing Eugene Seybold or the late Alice Roosevelt right now, she knew. But suppose she had seen them on the street the day before she met them? Would she have been able to describe them to someone later? For that matter, how did she know she *hadn't* seen them any number of times before? She didn't. They had just been invisible to her.

It was for this reason, she was sure, that Ella Cockrill had been able to exist for years as a homeless woman, practically under the noses of her wealthy family. Even though she was presumed dead, and had no doubt been legally declared so for some time to minimize inheritance problems for Emma and Eden, she had been able to come back to Palmer at some point and go undercover while she kept an eye on them. And on her daughter.

It hadn't occurred to Jackie, when she viewed Rosie Canty's effects in Cosmo Gordon's office the other day, that the page she had torn from the paper and carried folded up in her pocket had had some deeper significance for her than the issue of Farmers' & Growers' vs. Market Place. She had been so wrapped up in that debate herself that she had simply assumed Rosie had been concerned about it, too. If she'd been thinking at all, she'd have taken a look on the other side and seen the picture of Eden Cockrill— the real reason Rosie had kept the piece of newspaper.

Rosie had told Alice over and over that she was rich, and she would have been, too, if she hadn't jumped into the river and disappeared from the knowledge of her family. She would still have been seriously emotionally disturbed, however. Jackie couldn't see Ada and Felix Cockrill seeking out professional help for their daughter's dangerous instability—not if it meant that anyone outside the family would be made aware of the problem.

Was Ella's disappearance intentional, Jackie wondered, or had the accident caused her to lose her memory for a time? When people were as troubled as Ella Cockrill had been after she had signed over her newborn daughter to the tender mercies of Ada Cockrill, a trauma had been known to bring on amnesia. She remembered having read about it once. People who forgot themselves, it seemed, were often people who needed to forget.

What Ella had done after climbing out of the river might never be known, but at some point she had found her way back to Palmer—Eugene had mentioned that she'd been here when he arrived several years ago. By that time she had certainly known who she was—the name she had picked for herself said it as clearly as anything could: Rose was an obvious reference to Ada and her garden. Ella must have often felt like one of those unfortunate roses; pampered, fussed-over, trimmed back when she threatened to grow in an unexpected direction, always a victim of Ada's need to improve upon nature.

Frances had put the last piece in place when she remembered where she had heard the name Canty—a name that proclaimed its owner to be the poor twin of the true prince, or in this case, princess. Added to Cosmo's revelation of Rose Canty's real age, it had all become terribly and disturbingly plain. Ella Cockrill had come back to town, but never claimed her birthright. Now she never would.

Jackie and Jake walked up and down the dismal streets for over an hour, taking slightly different routes, but always coming back to the blocks between Ohio and Iowa streets that held All Saints and the Women's Shelter. At least while she was close to those places she felt as if friends, and help, weren't terribly far away. Nothing was happening around there, though, so after soaking up comfort from the

warm light coming through the windows onto the chilly
evening sidewalks, Jackie would always move on, and Jake
would follow, alert as ever to their surroundings.

As they walked across the street from the liquor store at
the corner of Third Avenue and South Illinois, about mid-
way between All Saints and the Women's Shelter, Jackie
noticed two men in dark clothing outside the store, smoking
cigarettes and watching people come and go. One of them
looked familiar. Jackie's heart thumped hard. Her knees
wobbled, but managed to hold her up.

She passed on without giving in to the temptation to
pause or turn her head, but turned into the nearest darkened
alleyway and looked cautiously back in the direction of the
liquor store. The tallest of the men was the one she had
seen talking to Felix Cockrill in the doorway of the council
chambers not two hours ago. She was certain of it. And
she was equally certain that that man had been Ivan Hahn,
Felix's ''contractor,'' whose primary job for Cockrill Industries seemed to be sending innocent people to the hospital.

She sank down on shaky legs to the ground, hunkering
beside a dirty brick wall in a dirty alley. ''Cripes, Jake,
now what?'' she whispered to her dog. Her bright idea
about disguising herself as a homeless woman and looking
for Felix Cockrill's thugs on the streets of Palmer had not
included a plan of action that would kick in if she actually
saw them. Poor planning, that. Maybe she should blow off
this amateur detective thing and go home and watch martial
arts movies with her son and his grandmother.

A man was coming out of the liquor store with a bottle
under one arm, visibly inebriated. Jackie knew it must be
against a whole handful of state laws to sell someone that
drunk another bottle of whatever he was drinking, but
where there was money to be made, some people tended to
wink at inconvenient legislation of that type. This man was
dressed in a torn overcoat that reached down to his ankles,
and he nearly tripped over the hem as he stepped down off
of the curb and made his way unsteadily across the street
toward Jackie and Jake's hiding place.

The men Jackie had been watching threw their cigarettes onto the sidewalk and followed him at a distance. Jackie pulled Jake back further into the darkness of the space between the buildings and held her breath while she listened to the three sets of footsteps getting closer and closer.

In the light rectangle formed by the opening onto Third Avenue, Jackie could see the man walking along the sidewalk. She clenched her fists and willed him to keep walking, but he stopped and turned into the alley, walking right past her. Jake was quiet but tense, ears standing forward, his eyes following the man's progress past them.

The two men following stepped into the alleyway. The shorter of them carried what looked like a length of pipe in his right hand. Jake let out a low, menacing growl, and the men wheeled around and saw Jackie and Jake. Jackie froze in terror.

The short man stepped forward, brandishing the pipe, and Jake went into action, pulling Jackie to her feet before she could let go of the lead. She opened her hand in time to keep from being propelled into the air, and Jake flew at the short man, snarling and snapping. The man moved surprisingly fast, dodging around a trash container and running away down the alley, still holding the pipe that had caused him to be attacked. Jake crashed into the trash bin and sprang to his feet, following at a gallop. They disappeared around the corner. The man they had been following got up and ran away.

The tall man—Ivan Hahn—looked in the direction his friend had gone, with Jake in pursuit, and started to follow. Jackie slipped along the wall, hoping to make it to the street before he could notice her and change his mind, but he was on her in two long strides, grabbing her upper arm in a grip that sent bursts of pain all the way down to her fingertips. "What the hell were you doing in here?" he shouted in her face. "That dog of yours is gonna kill Ernie!" He flung her against the bricks of the nearby building wall, knocking the breath out of her and slamming her head into the wall, hard. Her ears rang and her vision swam dangerously.

Ivan advanced on her again and lifted his arm up above

his head. "Stop right there," said a woman's voice from the direction of the sidewalk. "I've got a gun, and it's aimed at your back. Put both hands up, slowly, and step back."

Ivan raised his other arm and took a careful step backwards. Jackie looked out onto the street, expecting to see Bernie Youngquist, but it was Emma Cockrill who stood there, holding a chrome-plated revolver that looked enormous in her delicate hands. It also looked like it shot bullets the size of your thumb, and that evidently hadn't been lost on Ivan Hahn. He was visibly white as he stared down the huge barrel of Emma's gun.

Jackie got up slowly, holding her head. She didn't feel any too steady, but knew it was going to take more than one of them to handle this situation. "Just hold him right there for a minute," she told Emma. "I'll just go over to the liquor store on the corner and call the police."

"Oh, I don't care about him," said Emma. "Go on," she told him, "get out of here before I decide I'd rather shoot you."

Ivan Hahn didn't need to be told twice. He took off running down the street past the liquor store, and vanished around the corner.

Jackie watched him go in stunned disbelief. "I don't understand!" she wailed as she turned back to face Emma. "Why did you let him go?"

"Because I didn't come here for him," said Emma, leveling the gun at Jackie's midsection. "I came here for you."

CHAPTER 28

"Ella didn't threaten to kill herself if you ratted on her," Jackie said, hearing her own voice as though it came from outside her somewhere, "she threatened to kill *you*. She was much too aggressive to give up on life that easily, wasn't she?" She pulled herself to her feet and leaned back against the reassuringly solid brick wall, waiting for the dizziness to pass.

"I lied about that part," Emma admitted. "It seemed best at the time not to tell the whole truth. Ella was terribly angry. And terribly disturbed."

It runs in the family, Jackie thought through the fog in her aching head. "Did you lie about Timothy Burke, too? Did he really leave town to avoid facing his responsibility for Ella's pregnancy?"

"He sent her a note asking her to meet him. He said he wanted to marry her."

"But of course you got the note first?"

"I made sure she never saw it," said Emma. "I met him, pretending to be Ella. I was quite good at it, you know. I couldn't actually *be* Ella, with all her bravery and daring and disregard of the rules, but I could pretend to be for a little while at a time.

"I told him I didn't love him, and I never had. I laughed at his idea about getting married. I told him if he didn't leave town immediately, I'd report his conduct to the administration.''

Jackie watched Emma carefully as she spoke, waiting for the gun to falter, but it never did. She waited for Jake to come running down the dark alley toward them, but she knew Jake had cornered the man with the pipe and was probably holding onto his weapon arm with jaws that could crack a rib bone like snapping a doggie biscuit, and that his training would make him hold his man until someone relieved him. The problem seemed to be there was no one to do that.

"So Ella waited for Timothy Burke to come to her, and instead he went away."

"It was for the best," said Emma. "He wasn't good enough for her, and she was too much of a fool to see it. Mother would have agreed with me, though it might have been the only time in her life she would. We went home at the end of the school year, and Ella had the baby and signed it over to Mother. In September we went back to school."

"You told me Ella committed suicide that year. What really happened?" As long as Emma was talking, she wasn't actually shooting, and this was fine with Jackie. If she talked long enough, someone might come by and hear or see them. She was only hoping for a distraction, but she'd gladly accept a full-fledged rescue with no questions asked.

"She found out what I did—she guessed, really." Emma waved the gun for a brief moment, but not long enough for Jackie to feel confident about rushing her. "She never could leave the subject alone, and we were roommates, so I could never get away from it. It was always how she couldn't understand how Timothy could have gone away, and how she couldn't believe he'd treat her that way. It was tiresome at best, and maddening at worst, when she wore me down so with it.

"One night she was wailing about Timothy this and Timothy that, and she must have seen something in my face, and then she could tell, because I never could fool her about anything for long.

"Oh, how she raged at me!" Emma's eyes flashed in the streetlight, remembering her sister's anger. "She screamed about my ruining her life, and she took a pocketknife Daddy had given her—quite a sharp one—and chased me across campus and onto the high bridge over the river. It was night, and so dark—there was no moon.

"I tried to cross the roadway, but a car came out of nowhere around a curve in the road and nearly killed us both. I climbed up into the bridge supports, knowing she wouldn't follow because heights made her dizzy."

"But she followed you, didn't she?"

"She wanted to kill me. She would have killed me. She climbed up onto the bridge right behind me, and she struck out with the knife, and I grabbed her arm, trying to get it away from her."

"You grabbed her arm, or you threw her off the bridge? Which was it?"

"I was only trying to save myself! I didn't want to kill her! I grabbed the arm that had the knife. Her foot slipped, and she was hanging by the other arm. I tried to pull her up, but I wasn't strong enough. Her other hand slipped then, and then the hand I was holding slipped out of my grasp."

"And the body was never found, just like you told me today at lunch," Jackie finished for her. "But it wasn't over yet, was it, Emma? When did you know Ella was back in Palmer—when you and Eden saw her on the street that day she tried to talk to you?"

Emma nodded. "I knew Ella had come back to tell everyone what I'd done to her. I knew she'd come back for Eden, and I couldn't give her up."

"Ella had your father's love and even a bit of your mother's respect, and you couldn't have either one. She had courage and bravery, and a lover, and a child, and everything you couldn't have."

"I wanted Timothy Burke," Emma said, her voice dropping almost to a whisper. "I was in love with him before Ella had scarcely noticed he was alive, but I couldn't make myself approach him, and I hadn't the power to make him notice me. Ella didn't have to try to attract men's attention, you know. She only had to *be*. They did all the rest. Everyone loved Ella more than me. Eden would have loved her more, too, if she'd known her.''

"So of course you couldn't allow Ella to live, once you knew she was here in Palmer and knew how to find Eden. Did you know she'd been here for several years before you saw her?''

Emma looked genuinely surprised. "No," she said. "I didn't know. I often thought that she hadn't really died, because it seemed that if she had I'd have felt it somehow, as though a part of me were missing. The way I feel now," she said, "but when I saw her that day in the Market, when she tried to talk to Eden . . .''

"You knew you couldn't let her live?" Jackie prompted her.

"I didn't come down here to kill her," said Emma, shaking her head emphatically. "That only occurred to me later. I came to talk. We sat out in that alley behind that awful mission because I couldn't get her to go anywhere else. She was with that other horrid woman . . .''

"Alice Roosevelt?"

"That one. And I stayed back where it was dark until Ella had told her to go away. Then we talked.''

"And drank?"

"That Alice woman had left a bottle of liquor—vodka. It reminded us of the time we'd gotten drunk one night soon after we went away to University. Neither of us had ever touched liquor before, but we found someone who would buy us a pint of vodka, and we mixed it with some fruit juice up in our room. We only drank a little of it— we weren't drinking it very fast, and the headaches started after a while, awful, crushing headaches, and lasted all the next day. We were terribly ill.

"Anyway, we laughed about that, sitting in that alley, and I pretended to drink from the bottle and passed it over to her, and she said 'What the hell,' and drank some. I fooled her into drinking most of what was in the bottle, and she had no tolerance for it, of course.''

"Where was Arlo all this time?" Jackie wanted to know.

"She had him on a little chain at first, but then she took him off it, and put the chain in her pocket. She made him a bed from some newspapers that were in the trash bin, and put some more papers and cardboard down for us to sit on. It was getting cold—the storm was almost here.'' Emma looked up at the threatening sky above them and shivered.

"And when did he bite you?"

"Not until I pushed her into the trash bin," said Emma. "She was standing up by the open lid, and she looked as though she were ready to pass out. Suddenly it came to me that if I scooted under her and hoisted her up, I might be able to tip her into it, so I did. She started yelling at me to stop, but she was too drunk to do anything about it. That's when the dog jumped up off his newspapers and bit my leg. He savaged it, actually. He wouldn't let go, and he kept whipping his little head around and his teeth were digging deeper into my flesh. . . . When I tried to beat him away, he bit my arm as well. Finally I picked up Ella's backpack and kept hitting him with it until he stopped. I was bleeding so awfully!

"He followed me out into the street, but when I kept walking, he went back and sat by the trash bin. I went home, then, and waited. I knew she might die if it got cold enough in the night, but if she didn't, if she only got sick, I'd have to find some other way. Some more . . . direct way.''

"What danger was Alice Roosevelt to you?" Jackie demanded. "Wasn't killing one person enough?"

"I was afraid she'd tell someone she'd seen me after Ella was already dead," Emma replied.

"So you set the fire at the kennel," said Jackie. "And you tried to frame Alice for it by taking her earring and leaving it there.''

"Ella had told me she was fond of lighting matches," said Emma. "I was afraid of what would happen if the police should decide Ella's death weren't actually an accident. I know they were saying it was, but then there was all that talk about you solving crimes, and I thought perhaps you were investigating this one.

"I was afraid. If I could kill the dog, too, there'd be nothing to link me to the death of a homeless woman I never met. I still had Ella's backpack with some of her clothes in it. I pretended to be Ella one last time, and took the earring."

So in a way, Jackie thought, she herself *had* caused Alice's death, though she'd had no way of knowing that, and would have been helpless to prevent it. "You weren't taking any chances with Alice not being dead, though, were you? It wasn't enough to get her drunk and leave her to freeze—you had to crush her skull."

Emma shook just a little. The gun remained steady. "We were out behind some kind of warehouse on Second Avenue near the railroad tracks," she said. "There was a bin with broken pieces of metal. I found a heavy one. I had brought her a bottle of vodka. She was already drunk—already passed out. She never woke up."

Thunder deafened them, and a light like the sun split the sky open. Emma gasped and raised the gun. Without stopping to consider the wisdom of it, Jackie flung herself to the pavement and tackled Emma's feet as sheets of icy water descended on them, soaking everything in an instant. There was another roar, louder than thunder, as the gun went off.

CHAPTER 29

Jackie's ears rang painfully. She flailed about, blind and drenched to the skin, trying to reach the gun she couldn't see. Emma grunted in pain as Jackie's hand connected with the bandage on her arm. Her gun arm? Jackie couldn't remember. She held on anyway, squeezing the injured arm as hard as she could, gasping for breath in the dreadful downpour of freezing rain, and waiting for the sound of the next shot.

Emma's scream of terror accompanied another clap of thunder, and the accompanying flash showed Jake, jaws closed around Emma's wrist. "Don't move and he won't hurt you," she managed to gasp as she rose to her feet on shaking legs.

"He's already hurting me!" Emma shrieked.

"Oh, well, too bad then," said Jackie. "Don't move or he'll hurt you worse."

She steadied herself against the nearest building and took a deep breath while deciding if she was likely either to pass out or throw up. Neither seemed imminent. "Hold her, Jake," she told the Shepherd, who seemed hardly inclined to do anything else right now anyway. "I'll go across the street and call the cops."

"No need to go that far," said a woman's voice from behind her. "We're right here." Jackie turned her head and saw Bernie Youngquist, dressed in several soaking layers of old clothes and a torn knit cap, walking toward her, gun drawn and pointing at the pavement. Evan Stillman was close behind her, making approximately the same fashion statement.

Evan walked over to Emma and Jake, and reached down for the gun that was lying on the ground next to Emma's nerveless fingers. "Good work, Jake," he told the dog. "We'll just take this one off your hands, too." He slapped a pair of cuffs on the whimpering Emma and pulled her to her feet, while Jake stood by in case he might be needed again.

Jackie sagged against the wall, thinking that if it was all the same to everyone else, maybe she'd just pass out now after all. Bernie was beside her in an instant, lending support. "Are you going to be all right?" she asked, putting an arm around Jackie's shoulders.

"Yeah, I think so," Jackie said, giving the usually ravishing Bernie the once-over. "I think this grunge thing must be catching on," she told her.

"Evan and I were working undercover down here tonight trying to catch the men who were assaulting homeless people," she explained. "We heard some commotion over on Fourth Avenue and found Jake holding some guy who was convinced he was about to become a late snack for a German Shepherd."

"Good boy, Jake," Jackie said to her dog. Jake trotted over to her and put his nose in her hand, wagging his tail happily at the praise. "I should have trusted your judgment about Emma."

"As soon as we rescued that poor slob," said Bernie, "Jake took off in this direction. We cuffed his first perp to a drainpipe and followed him. We heard a shot on the way over. You're not hit, are you?"

Jackie shook her head. It hurt. "I've got a headache, though." She reached one hand up and felt the tender place on the back of her head. She could feel warm blood trickling under the cold, wet hair that was plastered to her skull. "Ivan Hahn and I had a little disagreement."

"Oh, yeah? And what do you call this," Evan asked,

pointing to the cuffed and unresisting Emma Cockrill, who hung her head in the pouring rain and shook with sobs, "a slight difference of opinion?"

"In a way," Jackie said, leaning gratefully on Bernie's arm. "I didn't think she ought to be going around killing people, and she didn't agree."

CHAPTER 30

"Can I see your stitches again?" Peter couldn't get over how cool it was that his mother had been beaten up by a criminal, spent a couple of hours in the emergency room, and was still standing on her own two feet. And she'd done it all wearing his clothes. "I'm going to tell my grandchildren about this one, no doubt about it," he said, examining the neatly shaved patch on the back of Jackie's head for at least the third time.

"Even my cousin the gangster can't top your mom the detective," Grania said to Peter. "Imagine wrestling with a murderer in a thunderstorm over a loaded gun! It's just the coolest thing I can imagine," she sighed, regarding Jackie with eyes that shone with admiration.

"I hope your imagination gets better before you get to my age," she told Grania, "or you might not get any older. Come to think of it, I might not myself," she added, stretching her aching muscles gingerly.

"Let's get you sitting down," said Frances, and Jackie was only too happy to accept the offer. Her mother and Tom fussed over her for a minute, and she found herself propped up on one end of the couch in her living room with half a dozen pillows behind her and a fuzzy green blanket over her legs.

"Peter's mother the detective needs to rest now, children," said Frances firmly. "I know she thrives on excitement, but even she has her limits."

"It's going to be fun figuring out what those are," said Tom Cusack, taking a seat on the edge of the couch. "At least I *think* 'fun' is the word I'm looking for." He looked tenderly at Jackie as he picked up her hand and kissed her fingers. "Whatever the word turns out to be, I'm looking forward to it."

Jackie smiled back at Tom. How did she get so lucky, she wondered. An ordinary man would have run away, screaming, long before now. But then Jackie would never have fallen in love with an ordinary man.

"I forgot to ask about the City Council meeting," she told her mother. "What did they decide about Farmers, and Growers' Market?"

"Well there was a lot of speechifying on both sides, of course," said her mother, sitting down in a nearby chair, "and a lot of presentation of facts and studies and dueling impact reports. In the end the Council decided to table the issue until next month's meeting. But I wouldn't worry too much about it—when it comes out that Felix Cockrill was paying thugs to beat up homeless people, he won't be able to get a doghouse erected in downtown Palmer, much less a seven-story commercial complex."

Jackie's nose tickled violently, and she pulled her hand away from Tom's and covered her mouth with it as a sneeze racked her. Her head started to hurt all over again. "Oh, no," she moaned. "On top of everything else, I think I'm coming down with a cold!"

"Peter, go run a hot bath for your mother," Frances instructed. "For a cold, darling daughter, we put you in a tub of hot water with Oil of Eucalyptus, and give you Vitamin C and lots of fresh garlic. You can't have too much fresh garlic when you're coming down with a cold, you know."

Tom smiled. "I guess I'd better kiss you now," he said. And he did.